ON PICKING FRUIT

ON PICKING FRUIT

a novel
ARTHUR WOOTEN

alyson books
NEW YORK

© 2006 by Arthur Wooten. All rights reserved.

Manufactured in the United States of America.

This trade paperback original is published by
Alyson Books
P.O. Box 1253
Old Chelsea Station
New York, New York 10113-1251

Distribution in the United Kingdom by
Turnaround Publisher Services Ltd.
Unit 3, Olympia Trading Estate,
Coburg Road, Wood Green
London N22 6TZ England

First edition: June 2006

06 07 08 09 00 a 10 9 8 7 6 5 4 3 2 1

ISBN 1-55583-952-5
ISBN-13 978-1-55583-952-9

Library of Congress Cataloging-in-Publication Data is on file.

Book design by Victor Mingovits.

ACKNOWLEDGMENTS

First and foremost to Joseph Pittman, Executive Editor at Alyson Books, who took a chance with an unknown novelist and put his professional trust in me and *On Picking Fruit*. Stephen Patterson for being a patient life coach, story editor, and dear friend. Ed Klein for being my creative cheerleader for almost thirty years. Bud Santora, who created the beautiful cover art for the original printing of *On Picking Fruit*. Traci L. Slatton for her inexhaustible belief in my writing abilities. Rita Jammet for her spirit and generous enthusiasm. Glenna Michaels for years of brilliant advice and encouragement. And last but not least my mom, Ronnie Wooten, who is my biggest fan and a source of endless "you can't make this stuff up" material.

FOR THE BOYS

CONTENTS

ONE

BORN FREE

I was born gay. That's what my mother always said. She'd tell the gruesome, gory details to any unsuspecting listener she could find. She especially enjoyed telling the story on my birthday. Well, the years that she remembered it, anyway.

Mother was way ahead of her time in regard to gay rights. If she could have, she would have shouted my sexual orientation from the rooftops. But she wasn't going to take the risk of not being heard and lose her voice screaming into thin air. No, she wanted a captive audience, and her pulpit of choice was our local supermarket.

We lived in the beautiful town of Bremerton, New York. Located in mid-Westchester, its claim to fame was that it boasted more former 1950s movie stars turned out-of-work game-show hosts than any other town in the county. And it was quite posh. A village full of overpriced white elephants clinging to the edge of our town's only industry, the Indian Ridge Country Club. Why they allowed us into Bremerton I have no idea. Don't get me wrong, I love my family and always will. But we were definitely the wrong people living on the right side of the tracks.

One particular birthday of mine that my mother did remember stands out vividly in my mind.

"Happy birthday, Curtis," she purred as we tore down Centre Street in our purple Ford Falcon, minus the muffler. (At

1

least we gave people a warning that we were coming.) "We have to get you a birthday cake."

I cautiously looked over at her, fearing where we were headed. It was the late 1960s, and she was wearing a silk head scarf with a gold-chain chinstrap, definitely designed not to blow away. She also had on big, black sunglasses, powder-pink lipstick, and long, dangly purple plastic earrings. And to top it off, she had clipped her signature piece, a wiglet, to the back of her head. However, none of this solved what my mother thought was the curse of the Jenkins clan.

"Darling, can you rearrange my falsie?" she asked as she took another drag from her Winston.

I crawled across the front seat and repositioned her bra cup. She yanked the rearview mirror toward her face. "It's crooked," she scolded as she juggled a right turn with one hand and adjusted the cup underneath the scarf with the other. "We're flatheads."

Yes, we were, and she wore falsies on her head to give it height.

Suddenly, the car came to a screeching halt in front the Purity Save More. I dreaded this, but before I could object, the lime-green halter top, coordinated madras clamdiggers, and espadrilles were a blur. She was out of the car and running into the grocery store, ready to start her story.

When I caught up with her, she had cornered Mrs. Brimblecom in the dairy case.

"I'm waddling my way down the hospital corridor to the bathroom, three weeks overdue with Curtis, my favorite son." She saw me shamefully approaching. "Here he is." She beamed with pride as she pulled me to her bosom, putting her hands around my head. "He was a humongous baby with a skull the size of a bowling ball."

A flat bowling ball, I thought.

"And he just didn't want to leave my womb. Who would

have? Would you, Tammy?" she asked.

Truth is, I would have run out if I could. The problem? I was stuck.

Mrs. Brimblecom made an escape.

"Wait, I'm not finished," declared my mother as she grabbed at her tartan-plaid skirt, causing it to rip.

Hearing the tear, my mother tore off toward the meat section. What she didn't hear was Mrs. Brimblecom calling her a bitch.

I caught up with her backing Miss Bricketto up against the link sausages.

"Angie, as I'm about to take a pee in the bathroom, some doctor ran up to me and yelled, 'If you go to the bathroom now, we'll lose both you and the baby!' "

I glanced away as Miss Bricketto looked to me for help.

"He hurled me onto a hospital bed and said, 'This is going to hurt you a lot more than it's going to hurt me, lady.' "

This is the part that stings, I thought as I scrunched up my face.

"And while I gripped onto the headboard, he reached inside of me with his bare hands and tried to turn my favorite one around."

Looking as if she was about to lose her lunch, Miss Bricketto broke free and made a beeline for the front door.

"It's a breech!" screamed my mother. "I had a breech!"

Good God, Mother, when was I born, the Dark Ages?

She zoomed over to the fruit section and trapped a portly young man in his twenties wearing a red hunting coat.

"The doctor couldn't turn Curtis around."

The man stared at my mother in disbelief as I caught up and hid behind her.

"He had to come out butt-first. And it was a big butt. They told me to hold on and they'd have my bulbous baby out of me in no time."

The man started to leave.

"*Wait*," she pleaded.

He turned around and looked at her with great annoyance.

"After fifteen gruelingly painful, uterus-tearing hours, out my Curtis came, ass first." She pulled me out from behind her. "And that's when I knew my favorite was gay. He was born free and just aching to show off his pretty pink butt to the world."

And I still am. It's my best asset. I'm the only person I know who was born and came out of the closet all in the same day.

"Well, what do you think of that?" my mother asked the young man proudly.

He took a moment, looked at me with disgust, and quite clearly said, "Faggot."

There was dead silence.

My mother may be eccentric. She may be a little over the top or even minus a few screws, but she also loves me and is fiercely protective. Like a tough cowboy straight out of a Western, she spread her legs and held her ground.

"What did you say?" she asked, as that vein that runs down the front of her forehead started to pulsate.

This time he whispered viciously, "*Faggot*."

In a flash, she reached for the closest ammunition she could find. Unfortunately for him, it was an unripe cantaloupe, and with all her might she hurled it straight at the guy, hitting him right between the eyes.

In an instant he was flat on his back. Leave it to my mother to knock out a redneck with a piece of fruit. Time stood still as my mother and I both digested what she had just done.

Nervous, she pushed me forward. "See if he's okay."

I knelt down, fearful that he was faking and that his hands would come up and around my neck and start strangling me, but he just lay there.

"Mother, he's not moving."

"We have to go," she said very calmly.

She grabbed my wrist and dragged me toward the front door.

"But what about my birthday cake?"

"I'll make you one."

I pulled away from her grip. "But you don't know how to bake."

She grabbed my hand again and pulled me with her. "Then you'll bake it, darling. You're good at that sort of thing. But if we stay here any longer, you'll have to plant a file in it and deliver it to me at the federal prison. Now get a move on."

We headed out the front door of Purity Save More with my mother declaring, "My Curtis is gay as a goose. And I love him for it."

I was ten years old.

≩ ≨

Three years later my mother gave birth to my baby brother, Stewie, and this prompted a plethora of questions from me about sex. Too busy to be bothered, she threw a book in my direction, *The Beauty of Reproduction*. This was her solution to telling me about the birds and the bees. Biologically, it explained everything. The man puts his penis into the woman's vagina, and then sperm from the man swim up the woman's uterus till one reaches an egg from her ovary, and they unite, and then a baby is made.

I was still confused. "But Mother, how does the sperm come out of the man?"

"Go ask your father," she snapped.

Now, my father was a brilliant scientist. He was socially unacceptable, but a genius. I think he invented plastic. But getting words out of him other than the square root of pi was like pulling teeth. So when I asked him how sperm comes out of a man, it wasn't a surprise to me that he started twitching and sneezing while running out of the room muttering something about the Big Bang Theory.

My mother always said, "It's a wonder we had you three kids, considering your father and I have only had sex three times."

It is true that I've never seen them touch or kiss, and they've always had separate bedrooms. They were good role models.

Two years went by and, still not knowing when or how thousands of spermatozoa were ejaculated from my male member, I came up with my own brilliant idea. The man must pee into the woman. Now, I know you're asking yourself, *Why didn't he just touch himself?* Well, it never occurred to me.

And for some strange reason, none of my friends filled me in on the confusing sperm mystery, either. Maybe that's because I had no friends.

But there was Peter Medina, the neighborhood delinquent. My mother threatened to kill me if she ever discovered I was hanging out with him. She was convinced he was the one who set the forest on fire behind our house and told the police I did it. The cops believed him, and now I have a record. And it's true. He did set it on fire and blamed me, but I forgave him because he offered to enlighten me to the pleasures of sex.

≳ ≲

One night, after tying his younger sister Delmadean up with extension cords, he dragged me up into his bedroom. He then subjected me to 8mm straight soft-core porn. It was very soft porn. You know, women in bras and panties taking baths in old-fashioned washtubs. Then he jumped up onto his bed, dropped his pants, got into doggy position, and told me to put my pud in his butt. It all seemed horribly unsanitary to me, but I always did as I was told when someone was holding a seven-inch bowie knife in his hand.

So I pressed my penis up to his buttonhole and pushed as hard as I could. I couldn't see what he was doing to himself, and I couldn't have entered more than an eighth of an inch when suddenly he moaned in ecstasy and then asked me, "Did you shoot it? Did you shoot your wad?"

Not knowing what he was referring to and frightened that he might shoot me with a gun, I answered, "I guess so."

"Good, now you can go."

Suddenly, his mother walked into the room. Frozen in our incredible position, she looked at us and screamed, "Damn you, Peter Medina! If I've told you once, I've told you a hundred stinking times. Don't mess up my good bedspreads with your damn muddy boots."

≶ ≶

Back in my kitchen, my mother was breast-feeding Stewie while rolling a joint.

"Baby, that Medina bastard is a bad influence on you," she said, gulping down a Schlitz.

I frowned disapprovingly. "Mother, I don't think it's such a great idea to smoke a joint and drink a beer while breast-feeding."

"Nonsense," she said as she brushed an ash off Stewie's face. "I did it while breast-feeding you, and look how swell you turned out."

I felt my stomach come up to my mouth. "You breast-fed me?"

"Sexiest thing I've ever done."

I gripped my stomach, resisting a dry heave.

She passed me the joint. "Here, take a toke. It'll calm your tummy."

I put it to my lips, inhaled, and doubled over in convulsive coughing.

"Now, Curtis, whatever possessed you to go up to that kid's bedroom in the first place?"

I grimaced. "A butcher knife?"

"Thank God you developed my sense of humor," she said, laughing, as she passed me the bowl of potato chips. "I love you, darling, but I swear I'll beat the living daylights out of you if I ever catch you poking your nose around that hoodlum again."

If she only knew that it wasn't my nose I was poking.

"I'm all for you being gay and all." She gave me the thumbs-up. "Hell, you were born gay."

"Yes, I know, Mother," I said, nodding. "I was born free."

"But can't you find yourself a new friend? One that doesn't torture domestic animals and has all ten fingers?" She switched Stewie to her other breast. "Someone nice and decent?"

"I'll try, Mother. I'll try."

≷ ≸

And that's when I met Ken.

My father the absent professor was not only brilliant, he also made a lot of money. I think he invented the ballpoint pen. The house he purchased in Bremerton was an extraordinary piece of property. A 1920s Tudor-style stucco house with more bedrooms and bathrooms than there were people in our house. Out back there was a clay tennis court, but none of us played. My mother used the net for drying laundry. Behind the tennis court was a cement monstrosity of a pool that had colored underwater lights. It was Olympic-size, with both one- and three -meter diving boards, but none of us swam. Out past the pool was the little house.

I took to sunbathing in the nude on the roof while lying on a raft. You know, the kind that had holes on the side so you could sip a glass and rest it while floating in the water.

Well, one summer day I was all lathered up with baby oil and lying on the float on the roof in the nude when I heard my mother screaming for me. I jumped up, slid on the raft, lost my balance, and fell back onto it with my talliwacker sliding right into the tight, warm hole meant for a tall, cool drink. I found out instantly how the sperm comes out of the man.

I named the raft Ken and fell madly in love with it. The two of us were inseparable, going at it three, four, even five times a day. I was making up for lost time. Boy, I had such a great tan that summer.

One day when I was rushing home to rendezvous with Ken, I discovered my mother burning something in the backyard.

"Stay away," she ordered. "Don't breathe the air."

Fascinated, I rushed to her side. "What are you doing?"

"That raft stunk to high heaven." She snarled, her lip curling. "Whatever was all over that thing, I'll never know. Must have been bacteria. I had to torch it."

I can't tell you how brokenhearted I was the day I found out that my mother had murdered Ken. She burned him at the stake, just like Joan of Arc.

After a proper mourning period, I did set out to meet new friends.

I had a tight but risky relationship with the cushions on the sofa. They were covered in plastic, so cleanup was a breeze. But family members had an annoying habit of walking in on us. One day my older sister, Kelly, caught us in a passionate interlude.

"Mother, Curtis is humping the couch again!" she exclaimed, wrinkling her nose. "You are such a disgusting pervert. I am never sitting on that thing again."

She turned on the television and sat down in the recliner, not knowing that we, too, had recently met and fallen in love.

And finally, one day I did discover my right hand. And to spice things up, I would switch to the left and pretend it was a stranger.

But it's Ken for whom I will always hold a special place in my heart. I loved that raft. I loved Ken unconditionally.

And although the relationships I had early on in my life were short-term and primarily with inanimate objects, the important thing is that they laid the foundation for my emotional and sexual maturity as an adult.

And now, at age forty-five, I'm a successful, available, physically buff New Yorker who's still searching, searching, searching for that ever-elusive man of my dreams. All I want is a smart, sexy, sensitive, single superman with a sense of humor. Is that too much to ask?

My therapist says, "In his earnest quest to find his true soul mate, Curtis is looking in all the wrong places."

My best friend says, "In his earnest quest for happily ever after, Curtis is much too selective."

My mother says, "In his earnest quest for a monogamous relationship, Curtis will sleep with anyone."

TWO

BEANO

As I came to, it was neither the oxygen tube coming out of my nose nor the needles jammed into my veins that frightened me. It was the face that scared me half to death. She had on too much foundation, too much mascara, and too much rouge, and she was much too close to my face for comfort.

She ran her fingers through my hair so sweetly, softly, and sensitively. But as soon as she had me, she snapped me back to reality by pulling it so hard I thought my scalp was going to bleed.

"Mother?" I managed to garble as I choked on my raw and parched throat.

"He's alive, Doc!" she screamed with delight while checking herself in her compact mirror and running out into the hallway. "My baby's alive."

I tried in vain to sit up but discovered that my veins were strapped down. What had happened to me? Why was I in the hospital?

Able to turn my head slightly from side to side, I could tell that I was in a single room. Either I was paying a fortune for this or I was in the ICU and paying a fortune for that.

And which hospital was I in? I focused on the color of the walls. It looked like an attempt at institutional green, but the result, was more like rancid sage. If something happened to me in my apartment on the Upper West Side, it would make sense that I would be brought to St. Luke's.

I strained my neck to see what was outside my window. There was nothing but blue sky. Was I even in New York City?

"Hello?" I feebly squeaked out. "Is anyone there?"

And then my lights went out.

≥ ≤

I'm not sure how long I was gone, but when I came to there was a male nurse staring at me.

"He's back!" she hollered.

Sorry, it was my mother. For the first time in a long time, I focused hard on her face.

She had been a beautiful woman, but decades of smoking, drinking, and overexposure to the sun had taken their toll on her. And unfortunately, after menopause she had started looking more like Mickey Rooney than Vivien Leigh; so with a giant nip here and a huge tuck there and a flap of something pulled up over her head, she was hot again. She neither looked sixty-five nor acted like it. Her silk blouse was a size too small, stretching buttons to the Nth degree, exposing her Victoria's Secret push-up bra.

I desperately searched my memory, trying to remember what could have possibly landed me in the hospital, when my mother decided to fill me in on all the minor details in her gentle and loving fashion.

"You tried to kill yourself, you big dope," she said as she applied another layer of her classic powder-pink lipstick.

"Kill myself?" I asked in disbelief.

She grabbed a tissue and blotted her lips. "You overdosed on a bottle of Beano and ruined my vacation to Atlantic City."

"That's awful."

"I know. I was planning that trip for months." She pulled eye shadow out of her purse and aggressively started to apply it.

"And then you go and slip into a coma."

Shocked, I tried to sit up. "A coma?" My head was spinning.

"Just for a day and a half."

She explained to me that my housecleaner had found me passed out on the bathroom floor of my apartment and that it was St. Vincent's Hospital in the Village that I was sent to because it's the one my doctor is affiliated with.

"But what caused me to go unconscious?"

She threw her eye shadow into her bag and grabbed my arm a little too roughly. "The doc said—and he's so damned cute, I might add—that you downed a bottle of Beano and they had to pump your stomach."

No wonder my gut ached.

She dug into her coat pocket, searching for a breath mint. "What the hell is Beano?"

I struggled to put the pieces together and informed her that it was an anti-flatulence pill.

"Darling? You must have inherited that from your father, because I've never farted a day in my life."

That's right, she always blamed it on the dog.

She ran to the door and looked both ways down the hall. "Where is the doctor when I need him?" She ran back to her purse, pulled out a bottle of Chanel No. 5, and doused her cleavage with perfume.

From out in the hallway, we heard a scream followed by a crash followed by a combination of swear words that I didn't even know could be put together. That had to be Quinn.

Quinn Larkin is my best friend. Actually, he's my only friend. I mean, I have acquaintances and people that I hang out with, but Quinn and I have history. We've been through the good and the bad together, and we're still speaking. That's probably because we've never had sex. And we're both comfortable with slapping each other in the face when necessary.

Frustratingly, he's accepted a soap-opera-writing job on the coast and, although we constantly speak to each other on the phone and meet up several times a year, he's missed terribly.

So, the fact that he traveled all this way to come to my rescue meant a lot to me.

He threw his bags into the room and looked back out into the hall. "Fuck you!" he shouted. "And watch where you're driving that gurney. You're supposed to heal people in hospitals, not kill them." He spun around. "Goddamned nuns."

Quinn not only acted devilish, he looked it, too, with his jet-black hair and emerald-green eyes.

He took one step into the room and tripped over his five pieces of Louis Vuitton knockoff luggage. Eccentric-looking he was; coordinated he was not.

"Oh, my," whispered my mother as she ran to his side.

He grasped her arm as she helped him up. "Mrs. Jenkins, you look fabulous."

"Thank you, Quinny," she said, trying to look demure. "You do, too."

Being a patient patient, I waited for Quinn to turn around and notice me plugged into a million machines, looking like Frankenstein.

But alas, he ran to the mirror in the bathroom and checked his face. "No, I don't. I just got off the red-eye, and that's exactly what I have."

She gasped. "You didn't eat the food, did you?"

He laughed, coming back into the room. "Hell, no. What do you think I am, stupid?"

It was then that he noticed my tray of food on the far side of the room, which obviously hadn't been touched. He proceeded to pick at what would definitely qualify as mystery meat.

"That shit on the plane will kill you," he continued. "I had a liquid breakfast. I had a champagne and another champagne and another champagne."

"Didn't you have any water?" asked my mother.

"Of course. I had two vodkas on the rocks. And I'm still bloated."

They should pump his stomach. My mother reached into her purse and pulled out a handful of blue pills.

"Here, take a diuretic."

"Thanks," he said as he popped it into his mouth.

Her face turned quizzical; no doubt she was wondering whether it really was a diuretic. My mother was a walking pharmacy.

"Mrs. J., how's life treating you up in Westchester?"

I felt an odd twinge of something bitter coursing through my veins, and it wasn't medication. Did Quinn like my mother more than me? I had absolutely lost all my patience.

"Hello!" I hollered in my recently developed Mercedes McCambridge voice. "I'm over here."

Quinn spun around, noticing me for the first time, and he actually seemed surprised. "Curtis, you look awful. What have you done to yourself?"

He swooped down toward me to give me a big hug but kicked the stand that held my saline drip, inadvertently pulling the IV out of my arm. The pain was excruciating, to say the least. The skin tore and my arm started to bleed.

Flustered, Quinn tried to shove the needle back into my vein. I blocked his hand. "You don't know how to do that."

"Just trying to help." Quinn backed away. "No need to snap."

"He's already snapped," whispered my mother as she grabbed some gauze and pressed it against my open vein.

Quinn looked like a dejected little boy. "Curtis, as soon as I heard that you were in a coma, I came running."

I reassured him that it was okay, but he continued anyway.

"And over the phone, I tried to convince the nurses that I was your sister."

He actually managed to make me laugh.

"But they wouldn't give me any details."

"Beano!" exclaimed my mother.

"You have flatulence, Curtis?"

I shook my head, wishing I had died. Or maybe I had and gone to heaven, because just then a tall, dark, handsome man in a white lab coat entered my room. Think Brad Pitt crossed with Keanu Reeves and you've got Dr. Reed Conway. This thirty something-year-old looked more like a character out of central casting than an internist.

"Jesus, Mary, and Joseph," muttered Quinn, scanning him from head to toe.

My mother gulped. "I'd drink his bathwater."

The two of them wrestled to see who could get to him first.

"Hello, my name is Quinn," he said, offering his hand. "I'm a single, successful Hollywood writer."

My mother hip-checked him out of her way. "He just writes for soap operas." She smiled and grabbed the doctor's arm. "Reed, what do you say you and I go down to the commissary and get better acquainted?"

He pulled away from her. "Actually, I'm here to see Curtis."

Quinn turned to my mother. "A hundred bucks says he's on my team?"

She challenged him. "You're on."

Reed looked right into my eyes and said in a deep, rich, velvety voice, "Curtis, thought we lost you there for a moment."

"Who are you?" I asked, hypnotized.

"Why, this is Dr. Conway, honey." My mother tried to slip in between us, but the doctor wouldn't budge.

"Curtis, I'm filling in for your primary-care physician, who's on vacation."

My mother chimed in again: "By the way, when you examined my baby, did you notice whether his left testicle has dropped yet?"

Embarrassed as hell, I felt my one good gonad shoot up into my throat.

"You can check *my* balls, Doc." Quinn smiled nervously as perspiration dripped from his forehead.

"And while you're at it, you can check my mother's, too," I added, glaring at both of them.

"Actually, I'm not a real doctor. I just play one on TV."

And with that, he slipped the IV needle back into my vein.

There was dead silence in the room as we all looked at him seriously.

"Joke?" He laughed. "A little ICU humor?"

Both my mother and Quinn giggled hysterically and drooled pathetically. He was a stunning man.

"Now why, pray tell, would a handsome, healthy hunk like yourself try to end your life with Beano?" asked the much-too-pretty doctor as he gazed into my eyes.

"Damn it, Quinn, you win," acquiesced my mother.

"I wasn't trying to end it with Beano—that I know." I strained to remember exactly what had happened. "What I do recall is that I woke up in the middle of the night from a vivid nightmare." I snapped my fingers as it all came back. "I was caught on the crest of a tidal wave with Barbra Streisand, who then turned into a snake that was trying to digest me in one gulp and—"

"Stop, baby," ordered my mother as she put the back of her hand to her head. "The dreaded dream-telling. He tortured all of us with this as a child."

I squinted my eyes and gave her a look that could kill.

"Go on, Curtis," encouraged the magnificent doctor, who sat on the edge of my hospital bed as he held and stroked my hand.

I focused hard. "I had just taken my first dose of Sustiva, a new HIV med that my doctor had put me on, and the next thing I remember, I reached for what I thought was Valium in what I assume was an attempt to kill myself."

"It's so embarrassing," whispered my mother.

"I beg your pardon?" I asked incredulously.

"Really, darling, it's one thing to take your own life; it's another to botch it."

"And with Beano, no less," added Quinn.

I looked at the two of them as though they were crazy.

She shook her head. "Honestly, Curtis, what am I going to tell my bridge partners?"

"Well, excuse me for living!" I screamed. "I know what you're thinking, Mother. I screwed up, again, unlike Dad."

Her jaw drooped. "What was that?"

"Dad succeeded in his suicide."

"Hold your tongue," she ordered as she held her chest. "Your father died a slow and painful death."

For a split second I thought I'd keep it in, but she had gone too far this time. "Mother, Dad was no fool. He knew from the get-go he had heart disease. He could have had bypass surgery, or lost weight, or even stopped smoking. But he did nothing but self-medicate himself to death. He wanted out."

And then it dawned on me. "What if this is genetic?" Suddenly, my heart rate rose and my breathing quickened.

"Calm down, Curtis," soothed Dr. Conway as he stroked my arm. "The new drug you took—Sustiva—has a hallucinatory affect on a small number of patients. In severe cases like yours, you probably had no real consciousness of what you were doing or why you were doing it."

I shot a glance over at my mother. "Well, I have plenty of consciousness now and I would love to try it all over again, but with the Valium."

"Don't say things like that, baby."

And then it happened. Her eyes got all misty. I wondered if this was a true, heartfelt emotion my mother was feeling, or yet another attention-seeking device.

"Curtis, I was just trying to maintain a sense of humor about all this." She actually started to cry and threw her arms around me.

And even though her quick glance to see if Dr. Kildare was catching every nuance was proof that this was yet another Oscar-winning performance, moments like this are rare between my mother and me. Soaking it up like a thirsty sponge, I held on to her like a baby, tears streaming down my face.

"I'm sorry, Mother."

"I love you, darling." She kissed my forehead. "You know that."

"And I love you, too," added Quinn as he started to cry.

"And I love you three," chimed in Dr. Conway.

There was a moment of silence, and then we all burst into laughter.

I managed to catch my breath. "So, you mean that I really didn't mean to kill myself, Doc? That it was the drug?"

"Most likely," he said reassuringly. "Have you been depressed? Anxious? Nervous?"

"Yes, I've been feeling all of the above," answered Quinn, raising his hand.

The three of us turned and looked at him.

Dr. Conway squeezed my hand, and I confessed that I had been feeling a bit stressed-out. But I wasn't aware of it being any worse than usual. "How soon can I get out of here?"

He patted me on the hand. "Let us do some lab tests and the paperwork, and as soon as you see the hospital psychiatrist, you can check out."

"Psychiatrist?" I asked grimly.

"Save your money, baby," warned my mother. "They're going to charge you a fortune and then try to brainwash you into thinking that I'm the reason you're all fucked up."

I shrugged my shoulders. "Okay, Doc, it's my mother's fault I'm all fucked up. I'm shrunk. Now can I go home?"

"Sorry, Curtis. Hospital rules. Anyone entering after an attempted suicide can't leave until we know they will be seeking professional help."

"Why don't you see my old shrink, Dr. Magda Tunick?" suggested Quinn.

We all looked at him.

"Yeah," he added, "I used to be a lot worse than I am now."

We couldn't help but laugh.

"She was great. So were the Ativan, the Valium, the Paxil, and the Doxepin. But you'd better hurry. Like I said, she's my old shrink."

"Yes, Quinn," I said. "We know you used to see her."

"No. I mean she's really old."

"Like how old, dear?" asked my mother.

Quinn shrugged his shoulders. "Like ninety-eight?"

"Damn!" exclaimed Dr. Conway.

"So she doesn't let you get away with anything. She doesn't have the time."

Again, the room broke into laughter.

"We'll have you out of here in a jiffy, Curtis," said the gorgeous doctor as he squeezed my hand. "What's this?" he asked as he looked at it. "Your lines are so rare."

"Are you a palm reader, too?" asked Quinn.

He traced my palm ever so lightly with his finger. "No, but we do know within the medical profession that this line here on most people breaks midway, but as you can see, on Curtis it transects straight across. You have what's called a monkey's paw. Your palm folds in half, which would allow you to hang comfortably for long periods of time from a tree."

"I knew my baby was special." My mother beamed.

I studied it. "Is this a bad thing?"

"It's one of the signs of mongolism," replied the doctor.

I pulled my hand away from all of them.

Quinn touched my head. "It seems only a bit larger than average."

"Dear, I've seen it swell on many occasions," informed my mother.

"Don't worry, Curtis. Your head is beautiful, and you're part of the one percent of the population who have the sign but are not affected." Dr. Conway winked at my mother and Quinn while exiting the room. "I'll be right back."

"Baby, let me look at that monkey's paw," she said, examining it very carefully. "What is it that I see here? Why, it's my favorite one and what's this? He's...getting married to a rich, young doctor named...Reed Conway."

Quinn looked at it. "Heavens, and you dare to wear white."

My mother threw me a mischievous smile. "Darling, fix yourself up before he comes back."

"And be aggressive," added Quinn.

"Quinn's right," Mother said as she kissed my forehead. "No time to be a wallflower." She pulled the oxygen tubes out of my nostrils. Damn, that hurt. "Make Mother proud." She licked her fingers and plastered down my hospital hair. "Ask him out to dinner. What's the worst he can do?"

"Say no?" I answered.

"Don't be so negative," she quipped, rearranging my pillows.

"Here comes lover boy now," whispered Quinn, as he peeked out the door.

"The two of you, get out of here now," I ordered as Reed reentered.

"Bye, Doc," cooed Quinn.

My mother squeezed his arm and winked. "Be gentle with him, Reed."

They left, and suddenly the room became frighteningly quiet.

"What a couple of characters." I laughed nervously as he wrapped a blood-pressure cuff around my biceps. I studied his fine, chiseled features as he held his stethoscope to my arm and pumped up the cuff. Certain that looking at him was going to make it soar sky-high, I looked away and asked, "Am I going to live, Doctor?"

"Sorry to disappoint you, but yes." He smiled warmly.

I took a deep breath and then jumped off the deep end. "Would you like to have dinner sometime?"

"No," he said, smiling even more warmly.

I was momentarily stunned by his quick answer. Trying to cover the awkward moment, I babbled on. "Is it a professional thing? Not having a date with a patient? In fact, if I hadn't been pressured"— he undid the tourniquet— "I probably wouldn't have asked you out at all."

I paused and waited for him to say something, anything. I literally heard his watch ticking. Or maybe it was my heart thumping. But Reed said nothing. So I listened to my instincts, promptly ignored them, and continued.

"So if it's an ethical thing and all, I totally understand you not wanting to date me."

"No, there's nothing ethical about it." He scribbled numbers onto my chart and slipped a thermometer under my tongue. "You're not my type."

"Oh?" I mumbled with an edge to my voice, which was actually disguising my fear of rejection.

"Curtis, I'm straight."

I swear I did a double take. "You're what?"

"You think I'm gay, right?"

"Well, it's not that you're effeminate or queeny or—"

"But you did think I was gay?"

I took the thermometer out of my mouth. "Yes."

He patted me on the back. "Good."

I was totally confused.

"Curtis, you know Nurse Eva?"

I had to think a moment. "The one who gave me the sponge bath?"

"Doesn't she have a great touch?"

"Yes, and quite warm hands," I added.

"Warm everything," the doctor whispered with an evil grin. "See, Eva and I are having a torrid yet secret love affair."

"Oh?"

"And I've just pulled through an ugly divorce. We're so in love, but we don't want anyone to know until she gets her divorce. All my friends, colleagues, and family members have been trying to hook me up with available women. Having said no to all of them because I'm just crazy about Eva, an awful rumor got started, that I might have turned...gay."

"Who started that?"

"I did."

This was stranger than fiction.

"And I'm happy as a clam to let the world think I'm queer."

"That way, no one suspects you and Eva?"

"I knew you were bright, Curtis," he said as he jotted down notes on my chart. "And I must say, you gay guys must be having the time of your life. I get hit on at least ten to fifteen times a day."

Lucky for you, I thought cynically to myself.

Dr. Conway started to leave and then turned back. "Say, Curtis? When you're feeling a bit better, would you mind going shopping with me?"

"For?"

"Clothes. I have no sense of style. Maybe we could go to Barneys and you could keep me looking gay?"

"Maybe," I said feebly.

"Thank you." He looked out into the hallway as a male colleague was walking by. In a loud voice he shouted back to me, "It's a date, Curtis?"

I tried to smile as he winked and left the room.

Good God, I've been reduced to a personal shopper for a

straight, gorgeous doctor who's pretending to be gay so he can continue his secret affair with a silicone-inflated, married Barbie doll of a nurse named Eva. Where's that bottle of Beano?

THREE

SHRINKING CURTIS

After setting up an appointment with Dr. Magda Tunick and realizing that the drama was over for the day, my mother and Quinn wasted no time deserting me. She shot back up to Westchester, and he hopped on the next plane to Los Angeles.

I had tried seeing a psychiatrist once before. Back in 1980, I helped a friend move up to Glenn Falls, New York. She was hired to be the summer-stock musical conductor of a regional theater in the picturesque Adirondack Mountains upstate. We met a friend of hers who was to be the leading man in two of the shows. He had arrived one week earlier and had already fallen madly in lust with a townie. After moving her luggage into her rented house, the four of us set out to have dinner.

The townie was neither shy nor discreet about his immediate feelings toward me. But I'm a sensitive kind of guy and didn't want to hurt the other man's feelings, so I flirted with the local only behind the actor's back.

Anyway, I was to leave the next day, taking a train out of Albany, which was an hour south of Glenn Falls, and, because my friend had already started rehearsals, the townie offered to drive me to the station.

And he did. It's just that it was a week later. I, too, had fallen madly in lust with him. He was a farmer and a carpenter and a chef and a poet and an absolutely perfect specimen of a man.

Curly brown hair, deep-sea-blue eyes, and bronzed skin, with a great personality. And, honestly, I knew he was crazy about me, too.

I had recently sold a treatment of a screenplay to a major studio, which gave me enough money to live on for the rest of the year. And by this time, Quinn and I had met and already become fast friends. He needed a place to stay, so I sublet my New York apartment to him, packed my bags, and off I went to live with my farmer in the Adirondacks, assuming it was for happily ever after.

There was one problem. Another player was involved in this man's life. But it wasn't the actor. It was his mother.

It turns out she was supporting him. Yes, he did run an organic apple orchard, but the profits were barely enough for him to live on.

She split her year living half of it in Dubrovnik, of all places, and half of it with him on the farm. To maintain her United States citizenship, she had to return every six months. This year she was to arrive on Christmas Eve.

I was crazy about my Renaissance man, and happy to spend the rest of my life with him, helping to plant the vegetable gardens and harvest the organic apples, hunkering down for the cold winters, all the while having great sex day and night and writing to my heart's content. And he was the romantic of all romantics. I was a happy camper.

She arrived mid afternoon and instantly hated me. I pulled out all the stops, being as charming and gracious as I could, but she was cold as ice. Turns out he had forgotten to tell her anything about me, not to mention the fact that I was living there, too.

Wanting his mother to like and accept me, I offered to cook a traditional English Christmas dinner of roast beef, Yorkshire pudding, and all the fixings. Well, I guess the farmer's mind was on something else, because he forgot to tell me that she was not only a Dane who hated the British, but that she was also a vegetarian.

"I don't eat anything with a face," she proclaimed in her thick Danish/Dubrovnik accent.

I had to figure out what to replace the meat with. I was stressed, to say the least. When I came up with the idea of a fondue, she was happy to remind me that I had my countries mixed up.

"Fondues are Swiss, not Danish," she said dryly.

When I found a salmon in the freezer and offered to whip together a creamy dill sauce, she acquiesced, saying she might pick at the fish. I thought I was quite resourceful. She was nonplussed, to say the least.

Once settled into the farmhouse, he joined her in the front upstairs bedroom, which was hers.

Around four o'clock I went up to knock on her door, but I heard them talking and laughing and decided to give them more time to catch up on things.

Come five o'clock, I had dinner ready and made myself a smart cocktail. I tiptoed up to her room and knocked on the door.

"Yes?" asked the farmer.

"Dinner is ready."

"We'll be down in a moment," he replied, and then I heard them giggle.

At five thirty, there were no signs of them coming downstairs.

At six o'clock I started my second cocktail and realized that I was mad. I was really mad, and feeling left out. I marched myself back up the stairs, banged open her door, and discovered them banging each other. They were having sex.

The rest of the details are very fuzzy, as you can well imagine. I do remember sitting in the living room, rocking to and fro, squeezing my toes so tightly that my feet started to bleed. I was told that, due to my overreaction, it would be best if I went back home to New York City.

During the car ride to the train station, I remember the farmer telling me calmly that what I had seen was very natural. That all children learn about sex from their parents. Once back in the Big Apple, I started seeing that first psychiatrist. To this day, I still believe that he thought I was making the whole story up. On my third and final visit, he asked if he could hypnotize me. I said yes, and he proceeded to sexually assault me. So it was understandable that I reentered therapy with great trepidation.

Up until now, I took great pride in thinking that I was a conscious, evolved human being who was totally aware of his actions and reactions in life. For the most part, my therapy was writing. But obviously, at this stage of the game, I needed some outside help.

≥ ≤

It was a spectacular spring day in New York City as I walked over to the new shrink's apartment, located on Riverside Drive. The temperature was warm enough to wear a light cotton jacket. The daffodils, tulips, forsythias, and dogwoods were in full bloom. Although it's truly a wonderful time of the year in the city, I found this spring to be unsettling and full of melancholy. Who knows why, but this season I sensed more than ever how incredibly short-lived these beautiful manifestations of nature were.

What brought me back to reality was the way people were looking at me as I walked down West 76th Street toward the Hudson River. I wasn't being paranoid, but each and every one of them looked me up and down and then smirked. Did they know I was seeing a shrink because of an unconscious suicide attempt? Did I have *loser* written all over my face? Did my gait tell the world I was a failure? Could little children even detect that I was a basket case?

"Hey, mister," giggled a toothless boy, "your fly is open."

Leave it to a child to be totally honest. Relieved that that was all it was, I zipped up fast and took a left onto Riverside.

I almost stepped on a bag lady who was sitting on the sidewalk. I've seen her on a regular basis in different parts of my neighborhood for the past thirteen years. In fact, if I didn't see her, that's when I would worry. Her head was shaved bald, probably because of head lice, and her skin was as brown and leathery as an old shoe. Every time I passed, she asked the same question.

"Any change, sir? Any change today?"

As always, I grabbed whatever coins I had in my pocket and dropped them into her cup, whispering to myself, "No, ma'am. No change today. Same old same old." After all these years, I still got a kick out of the pun.

Quinn's ex-therapist's apartment was in an old, run-down, four-story brownstone. Ivy covered the entire front of the building, while three-foot weeds sprouted out from the wrought-iron fence.

Outside the front door were buzzers for tenants, one for each floor.

Dr. Magda Tunick Floor #3

As I pressed the black button, I had thoughts of Lurch answering the door. After hearing a faint click, I pushed with all my might to open the heavy cracked-glass and metal door.

Once inside the foyer, I realized how special this building was. Although tenants lived on different floors, the original house was still intact.

As I started up the rickety staircase, I wondered who was older: Dr. Magda Tunick or this house. Even the air smelled old. Like a combination of dying flowers and beef stew.

As I passed the second-floor parlor door, I heard it creak

open. When I stopped to look, it slammed shut.

I reached the third floor and was just about to knock on the door when I heard a high-pitched growl from inside.

"Get away, Emily-Mae," shouted a voice with a thick Eastern-European accent. "Get away." Then I heard what sounded to me like a swift kick and a sharp yelp. "Who is it?"

I cleared my throat. "Curtis Jenkins?"

"You're late," she scolded.

I looked at my watch. I was late by maybe a minute or two.

By the time Dr. Magda Tunick slid open her massive oak door, Emily-Mae—whatever she was—was out of sight.

"Come in. Don't have time to waste."

I didn't realize that I had a preconceived idea of what she looked like until I saw her. Instead of a tiny, frail woman, Dr. Tunick stood at least six feet tall. She showed no signs of osteoporosis and was probably the same height she had been at the age of sixteen.

She was a strong woman with long, rather shapely legs. Her white hair was braided and circled around her head like Maria von Trapp. But what she maintained in height, she definitely lost in facial hair. Looking as though she had used a piece of charred wood from the fireplace, she'd charcoaled her eyebrows on rather carelessly. And if she were ever in a contest with Lucille Ball to see who could paint their lips out the farthest, Dr. Magda Tunick would have won hands down.

"You sit there," she ordered, pointing to a small cloth-covered chair.

I took off my jacket and folded it over the arm of the chair as she sat down in an overstuffed chair opposite me.

Because it was early afternoon and bright out, my eyes had trouble adjusting to the dimness in this parlor room. There were heavy red-velvet draperies covering her front windows. I sensed that the overall décor dated back at least to the early 1930s.

Next to Dr. Tunick was an ancient mahogany table with a

box of tissues and a lamp on it. She reached over and clicked it on. It was one of those fascinating globe lights with hand-painted designs. The first click turned on the top globe; the second click turned on the bottom. Her third click turned them both on. I wanted it.

"Why are you here?" she barked.

I sat at attention. "Hospital orders."

She riffled through her papers and grunted. "Right. Attempted suicide."

"And Quinn is my best friend," I added.

She put down the papers and looked at me. "I see we have a lot of work ahead of us."

"I beg your pardon?"

She crossed what looked like a ten-foot-long right leg over her left and then started to rotate her ankle aggressively. Her feet were enormous. I wondered if I could fit into her shoes.

"Couldn't crack his nut, so I fired him."

I looked at her, confused.

"You fired a patient?"

Without answering, she went back to studying the paper-work. Her gigantic foot was spinning from her big, thick ankle, fast as a propeller. I wondered if she was actually a man.

Suddenly, there was a loud crash and out of a back room, a batlike gargoyle creature with needle-sharp teeth came charging right at me.

I screamed as I pulled my feet up underneath me.

"Emily-Mae!" shouted the doctor.

Upon hearing her voice, the thing veered to the left and smashed right into an andiron in the fireplace.

"My dog."

I looked in disbelief. "That's a dog?"

Dr. Tunick picked up the stunned canine and placed her on her lap.

"A Brussels griffon."

That's easy for her to say.

"She's blind."

"I'm sorry." I held my hand out to her, hollering, "Here, poochie."

"And partially deaf," she added, while looking at her watch. "Let's get down to business. There are things I need to find out about you."

≷ ≷

It seemed as though it took hours for Dr. Tunick to ask me the million and one tedious questions about my life, starting with the success of my writing career and ending with the failure of my love life. It was Emily-Mae's snore that woke me up.

She looked at her legal pad and reiterated, "You don't like porn. You don't go to dirty bookstores. You don't go to the baths. You don't have sex in public places. You don't do drugs. You aren't interested in group sex. You're not into S and M or anything kinky. You're not a voyeur. And you're not an exhibitionist?"

"No."

"Let me ask one more question, Curtis."

"Shoot."

"Are you gay?"

"Well, of course I am," I said proudly. "I was born gay."

She paused and wrote something down with her massive hand. It surprised me that at her age, there seemed to be no gnarling of the knuckles. The hand was so large and manly. I wondered to myself, if she were to slap me across the face, would my cheek be large enough to hold the imprint of her hand?

"Curtis, are you with me?"

I broke away from this disturbing daydream and looked up

at her face. *Why in God's name did I ever think of something like that? I must see a professional about this.*

She looked me straight in the eye. "Do you know what you are?"

I shook my head.

"Boring."

"I beg your pardon?" I asked, shocked.

"No wonder your love life sucks."

I shook my head in disbelief. "You can't talk to me like this."

"I can honestly say that I believe that your suicide attempt was drug-induced. But what this session has brought forth is a man who is terribly lonely and definitely depressed. Do you know why you are depressed?"

Without even being aware of it, I crossed my right leg over my left and started twirling my foot around my ankle. "I've worked so hard on my career, and I have all these wonderful things in my life. I guess it might depress someone if they had no one special to share it all with."

"You aren't in love, and no one's in love with you."

I stood up and started pacing the room. She was making my life sound so bleak.

Dr. Tunick shouted at me like a drill sergeant. "Sit down!"

I did as I was told.

"You're handsome, successful, single; you're a real catch. What's the problem?"

I threw up my arms and said sarcastically, "I don't know, you tell me. You're the shrink."

She didn't laugh.

I explained to her that my work is very isolating. I write all day, by myself. I talk to and occasionally meet my agent or editor. I don't know where to meet men. I've spent all of my adult life focusing on my career. I just haven't paid much attention to my love life.

She shifted her angle. "Curtis, how do you create a play or a book or a screenplay?"

I shrugged my shoulders.

"What's the first thing you do?"

I pondered it. Ideas come to me in many different ways. Inspiring me to put them together, until they—

"I can tell you're thinking too hard. The bottom line is that you picture something in your mind and then you make it physically manifest. Ideas turn into words, which turn into books, plays, or movies."

I nodded.

"It's the same thing with finding a significant other. Picture what you want and whom you want, but just make sure you are very specific. Don't leave any details out. And be careful of what you ask for, because you'll get it."

"But, Doctor, you can't just imagine the perfect man and—poof—there he is."

"If you imagine a gay man, you'll get a poof."

There was a moment of silence, and then I blurted out a laugh.

She remained deadpan. "It's a universal law of cause and effect."

She was tough, and this was virgin territory. I was out of my element and feeling the heat. Beads of sweat formed on my upper lip. Searching for something, anything, to say, I delightfully discovered a large hangnail on my left thumb and proceeded to self-destructively pull at it.

She continued. "What's one of the most important qualities you must have in a mate?"

I went through a long list in my mind. "Honesty?"

"Is there someone in your life who has been dishonest to you?"

"Every man I've ever dated." I forced a loud laugh and pulled harder at my hangnail.

She looked irritated, rubbed her temple, and then moaned.

"What does your moan mean?"

She shifted uncomfortably in her seat, making sure not to wake up the dog. "Nothing."

"Yes, it does. It had a judgmental tone to it."

Dr. Tunick rolled her eyes. I sensed that she had had just about enough. Then it dawned on me that if I kept this up, maybe she would fire me, too.

She looked back down at her notes. "Curtis, you spoke earlier of a complicated relationship with your mother."

Annoyed at the question, I shook my head. "It's not complicated. I said it's simple. Simply dysfunctional."

"How so?"

I took a deep breath. "Can I stand up?"

"If you have to."

It felt good to stretch my legs. The chair she had me sitting in had cut off the circulation in the back of my legs, causing pins and needles.

"The problem with her is that she dresses too young. She wears too much makeup. She wants to party all the time and hang out with people thirty years younger than she is."

I wandered over to the fireplace on the far wall and quickly wiped my hand along the mantel, checking for dust. I set off a minor dirt bomb and sneezed twice.

"It sounds like you're being judgmental of her."

I spun around. "Whose side are you on?"

Dr. Tunick put both hands up in the air. "I'm not on anyone's side."

I continued to walk around the room and discovered a tea cart with an ornate, unpolished silver tea set, a hunter-green velvet divan, and an antique pump organ in the far corner. I settled in front of some poorly lit, faded diplomas on that wall. "My mother's nosy." I squinted as hard as I could but could only make out words here and there, like *University, Tunick,* and *Honorary*. "She has to know everything I'm doing. When I'm doing it. Whom I'm doing it with." I stopped in front of a picture of a very tall, lanky young woman and a very attractive man. "Is this you in the picture?"

"Please sit back down." She observed me a little too carefully as I crossed the room and took my seat. "Could it be your mother was just being maternal?"

I unconsciously started on the hangnail again. "She's not looking out for me. She just doesn't want to miss out on the fun."

Dr. Tunick took a note. "Have you set boundaries for your mother and told her to respect them?"

I laughed to myself. "That's like asking a one-year-old to color within the lines."

Dr. Tunick shot a quick glance at her watch. "Do you feel she is being dishonest?"

"I don't think she's always honest with me."

"How so?"

"Well, for example, the premiere of a play that I had written opened in Key West a few years back. Now, this piece is my baby. In fact, I refer to it as my love letter to my family."

"In other words, you stole their lives and put them up on the stage for people to laugh and cry at?"

"I see you've been speaking to my mother."

Again, Dr. Tunick didn't laugh.

I continued. "I hadn't seen her in almost two years, and lipodystrophy from the HIV drugs I had been taking had literally destroyed the fat cells in different parts of my body. The once cherubic face her favorite child had had was now hollow and gaunt."

The doctor breathed a heavy sigh. "Do you have a Peter Pan complex?"

"No, of course not."

I took my time explaining to Dr. Tunick that that wasn't

the point. I was so frightened of what my mother's initial reaction would be to my face that I focused on my body and what I would be wearing. It took me weeks to find the perfect outfit and months to pay for it. A beautiful black silk short-sleeved shirt and black pants that fit so well they looked like they were hand-tailored. Then I ran off to the gym and pumped up my body. And when the moment came, when we met in front of the Waterfront Playhouse, where my play was up on the marquee and my name was in lights, she barely even noticed my face. Instead, she looked at my body in my carefully picked-out and priceless outfit and said, "Darling, you look just like Jack LaLanne."

A few seconds went by and Dr. Tunick uncharacteristically doubled over in hysterical laughter. Her timing couldn't have been worse.

"Don't laugh at me." I pouted. "It's not funny."

She continued to laugh as she grabbed tissues from the table next to her.

I was infuriated. "What my mother said to me was awful."

Dr. Tunick looked down at my legs as her laughter turned to concern. She handed me the box of tissues.

"What's this for?"

She gestured to my pants.

I looked down. "Shit."

The left thigh of my pants was splattered in blood. I had torn the hangnail off and removed a major chunk of skin with it. The stinging, self-inflicted wound hadn't even registered its pain at first. I wrapped my thumb in tissue. "I'm okay." I laughed, holding up the thumb. "Just a bad habit of mine."

Dr. Tunick furrowed her charcoaled brow. "Curtis? Could it be that your mother was being honest?"

I took a long pause and with great resignation said, "Possibly."

"Obviously, you are still seeking approval from her, and

every time you expect it and don't get it, you will be disappointed."

"So, now what?"

She gestured to me. "What do you want? What's missing from your life?"

I thought long and hard. "First and foremost, a man."

She looked at her watch. "Okay. If you want to continue working with me, I suggest you have a minimum of one date per week, and we will see each other every two weeks until you find a man. Is it a deal?"

I paused as she looked at me impatiently.

What was I getting myself into? With great hesitation, I replied, "It's a deal."

"Good. I want you to keep your eyes, ears, and heart open. I want you to meet people on the street and at the supermarket. Look at personals in magazines and online. I want you to tell every friend you have that you are ready to meet the man of your dreams. Is that understood?"

"Yes, sir."

She looked at her watch again.

"I know why you do that."

Dr. Tunick slipped notes she had taken during my session into a folder. "Do what?"

I sat there feeling quite clever as I grabbed my jacket from the arm of the chair. "Look at your watch so much."

She sat there, not even qualifying the statement, so I continued.

"Quinn said you are ninety-eight and you have no time to waste."

The doctor made a funny "tish" sound with her mouth. "Quinn doesn't know squat."

"You mean you're younger?"

I looked down and hadn't realized that at some point, she had slipped one of her giant shoes off.

"Curtis, who lies about their age?"

"Gay men?" I desperately wanted to slip my foot into it.

"True. Who else?"

"Women?" I knew it would fit.

Sensing my stare, she put the shoe back on. "If a woman dares to tell you her age, you always add at least three years to it."

I looked up at her face. "That makes you a hundred and one?"

"At least," she admitted, looking at her watch. "But the real reason I'm looking at my watch is because your time is up."

With that, we both stood and Emily-Mae tumbled to the floor. She sensed I was still there, and although she bared her teeth at me, she was facing the wrong direction.

Dr. Tunick shook my hand as we walked to the door.

"Same time, two weeks from today?" she asked.

"Yes," I agreed, looking up at her. Damn, she was tall. "And at least two dates to share."

Emily-Mae growled as the Dr. Magda Tunick opened the sliding door.

"She likes you, Curtis."

"How can you tell?"

"Because she just peed on your shoe. Good-bye."

She closed the door as I looked down at my yellow-stained sneaker.

FOUR

DESI AND LUCY

I couldn't wait to tell Quinn and my mother about the mission Dr. Magda Tunick was sending me on. But in my gut I felt that if I did, instead of sharing information, it would be like supplying them with ammunition.

The next morning, I left my apartment building with my eyes open, ready to meet the man of my dreams. Maybe I'd bump into him in my elevator, or on the sidewalk, or at the bank. Or perhaps it would be on the subway headed downtown to my gym on Sixth Avenue and 19th Street.

I always chose gyms for the basics, and this time it was Bally for the masses. When I purchased the membership back in the 1980s, it was locked in at the lifetime price of $62 a year. I believe they told me it was for my lifetime or theirs, whichever expired first. That came to $5.20 a month, and I went every day and they hated me.

I take my workouts at the gym seriously. Unlike a lot of other men, I'm neither a voyeur nor an exhibitionist. I use my workouts to sedate my brain. The icing on the cake is that they keep me in great shape. And people at my gym have come to realize that I'm not there to socialize. My workouts, like my sex life, are quick but intense.

And the few people who I have befriended understand one of two facial expressions I have while working out. Either yes, I'm approachable today and we can chat but just for a bit, or stay away, my time is short.

I've also become very weary of people asking me how gay my gym is. Many want to know how often the guys pick me up and what kind of activity goes on in the showers and the sauna. Truth is, there was so much fucking going on in the saunas that they closed them down. That pisses me off. Personally, I used to like taking a sauna after my workout.

And when I work out, I don't sweat. Go figure, it's a glandular thing. I wear my workout clothes to the gym, and therefore no one sees me naked. I'm not going to stand in the locker room or shower or in front of the sinks and stare at my naked body in the mirrors. And I don't want gays, bisexuals, or (more often than not) straights gawking at my body. They have to earn the right.

That's another thing. I have a hard time telling whether the men in my gym are gay or not, because all the straight guys dress like us. The earrings, the shaved heads, the goatees, the shell pants, and the pierced nipples peeking out from skimpy tank tops. So, to simplify my gym life, I keep to myself. Therefore, no one ever has and no one ever will pick me up at the gym.

"Hello," he whispered into my ear as I did a shoulder press. And with that, I was picked up.

Magda's technique was working.

"Hi," I stuttered, as my astigmatism struggled to see whose face was in mine. Don't ask me why, but I hate to wear my glasses while working out.

After twelve years of respectfully acknowledging gym buddy number 204 with a nod, a flick of finger, or a grunt, we finally communicated verbally to one each other.

I had always wondered who this elegant and refined man was. Maybe a professor at Columbia who had a seven-room Upper West Side apartment with a study that was paneled in deep, rich woods, cocooned with floor-to-ceiling built-in bookcases stocked with volumes I'd never read? Or maybe a Wall

Street banker who loved sipping single-malt scotch whiskey while doing the *London Times* crossword puzzle in ink, in front of a roaring fireplace at his beach house off-season in the Hamptons? Or maybe...I was describing myself?

"I've been wanting to say hello to you for years," he said in a deep, breathy voice that took my breath away.

I responded very eloquently: "Okay."

I had to regroup fast. This guy was in a different league. I hurled myself into my workout. Focus and concentration were my strong points. Nothing throws me while I'm working out, thanks to years of gymnastics, junior high through college. I grabbed hold of forty-pound dumbbells, hooked my legs around the support on the reverse-incline bench, and slowly lowered my body down, my feet higher than my head. I raised my weights straight above my chest, took a deep breath, and that's when I noticed that my new, old friend was standing directly behind me.

Sporting gold running shorts that slit all the way up to his hip bone and with a barbell behind the back of his neck, he proceeded—for my benefit—to do a set of deep squats dangerously close to my face. On his third rep, my arms began to tremble and I dropped my weights.

This never happens to me. I was losing control. I could hurt myself. So I ran to the water fountain to regain my composure. Lips wet, I spun around, and there he was.

"What's your name?" he asked.

"Curtis," I gurgled in my deepest, most masculine voice, which I save for answering the phone. Four out of five solicitors respond to me with a, "Hello, ma'am. May I speak to your husband?"

"Candace?" he asked quizzically.

"No, Curtis," I exclaimed.

First I had to speak in the right register. Now I had to take elocution lessons?

"Hi, Curtis." He held out his hand. "Desi here."

Confused, I shook it. "Dizzy?"

"No, *Desi*."

I tried to pull away, but he wouldn't stop shaking my hand. He continued to explain. "It's short for Desifinado."

Finally I got my hand back. "What an unusual name." I wracked my brain thinking of what origin that might be. "Greek?"

"Greek my ass." He laughed.

I'd be glad to. I thought to myself.

He pulled me to a far corner of the free-weight room. "I'm French and Colombian and can speak seven languages."

I was scared. "And what is your last name?"

"I don't have one," he said proudly, lifting his chin up into the air. "My name is just Desifinado."

"Like Charo?"

He corrected me, reaching out for my hand. "Like Cher." He started massaging it. "Curtis, you're a very beautiful and powerful man. It's time we had tea," he declared.

I pulled my hand away. No one had ever picked me up with a line like that before. Tea? Did this mean he didn't drink? I don't trust anyone who doesn't drink alcohol. But then again, it was only three in the afternoon, too early for even me to start.

"Tea it is," I agreed, as if it were the most natural suggestion in the world. I'm much too flexible.

"I'm done with my workout; are you?" he asked with a smile that implied much more.

I lied. "Yes." My workouts are quick, but this was ridiculous.

"You taking a shower?" he asked with a wink.

He was getting into dangerous territory. "No, you go ahead. I'll lift a little more and give you time to do your thing."

"Join me in five minutes?" he asked as he scooted into the men's locker room.

The last thing I wanted to do was walk in on him standing there stark naked, so I played it safe and gave him ten minutes. Then I went into the locker room and there he was, standing stark naked, admiring himself in the mirrors.

I am so repulsed by this behavior and at the same time attracted to it. I'm sure Dr. Tunick will enlighten me to the fact that this is a form of disownment, and what I'm truly aching for and need to satisfy is an uncontrollable urge to be arrogant and cocky and strut around buck naked in a public place. I don't think so.

Wanting to gaze at his tanned, naked, and incredibly sensual body—yet frightened to death that I would come off crude, crass, or (heaven forbid) interested—I chose to focus intensely on his eyes, which were a deep chocolate-brown.

At this moment, the French and Colombian Adonis reached for a woman's compact mirror, unself-consciously opened it up, and checked the back of his head. What in God's name could he be looking for? He had a full head of salt-and-pepper hair. But maybe it was too full. Totally embarrassed, I looked away.

Outside the gym, we walked west on 19th Street.

"I know of a charming little coffeehouse around the corner on Eighth," suggested Desifinado.

"Not—"

"The Dixie Cup."

I was *afraid* he was going to say The Dixie Cup. The one place I avoid with more passion than the locker room showers is The Dixie Cup. It's cruisier than the Westside Baths, not that I would know. I truly hate The Dixie Cup.

"I love The Dixie Cup," I said. "But won't it be too crowded?"

In fact, it's usually so crowded that I cross the street rather than try to force my way through the hordes of steroidally bulging local gym rats and the drooling out-of-towners worshipping them on the sidewalk.

45

"Don't worry," Desi said, slipping my arm through his. "I have my own table." He patted the top of my hand ever so condescendingly. "Talk to me, Curt. What do you feel compelled to tell me?"

Dramatically, I pulled my arm away from him. "I feel compelled to tell you that my name is Curtis, not Curt."

"Don't people call you Curt?"

"Only once."

We stopped in front of the gay coffeehouse.

"But I like Curt. And you will call me Desi," he declared as the parting sea of gay men opened up and sucked us into The Dixie Cup.

"I'll have a grande skim latte with an extra shot of espresso," ordered Desi to the young-enough-to-be-my-son Chelsea boy. He was decked out in this year's uniform, which consisted of a cotton orange sleeveless T-shirt, beige capri pants, and mules.

"And I'd like the French vanilla Colombian espresso cappuccino."

"Wouldn't we all," said the counter boy while winking at Desifinado.

"Let's sit," Desi said, drinks in hand. "I have some serious things to discuss with you."

"Serious?" I asked, totally thrown. And lo and behold, he did have a table waiting for him. I was truly scared.

"I have to ask you again, Curt, what do you feel compelled to tell me about yourself?"

"Okay, well, first that I'm forty-five years old and—"

Suddenly, Desi slipped his hand into mine and I became speechless. It felt so warm, so safe, and so sincere.

"Thank you," he said profoundly.

"For what?"

"For being you," he said with a smile that made my toes curl. "Forty-five is perfect; I love older men."

"How old are you?"

"Forty-four, Curt."

I'd rather he'd called me Candace.

"Why now, Curt?"

Desi looked so deeply into my eyes. "Why now what?"

"After twelve years, why are we having tea now?"

The only thing I could think to say was, "Cause you asked me to?"

"No. When you want something bad, when you want it with all your heart, the universe will conspire to make it happen. I've been watching you for years. Your workouts are so graceful and your body is so exquisite. We were meant to meet today. Aren't you glad I'm single again?"

Having said that, he reached across the table and wiped my mouth with his hand. Fearing I had French vanilla Colombian espresso cappuccino on my mouth, I pulled back.

"Do I have something on my face?"

"No. I had to touch your lips. I love the way they move when you speak. I just had to feel them."

Flustered and mildly disgusted, I managed to smile. "You're such a smooth talker, Desi."

"In seven languages," he reminded me. "Look at your face."

I was afraid he was going to take out his compact.

"Your whole face smiles, not just your mouth. Your hazel eyes, your crooked nose, your high forehead. Even your curly brown hair."

Desifinado thinks my hair smiles? This was getting weird. And what was going on with his hair? His widow's peak was just a little too thick-looking.

"Curt, you felt compelled to tell me you are forty-five." Desi tapped the table with his fingers and smiled slyly. "Anything else?"

I honestly couldn't tell where he was going with this. I thought hard. "I'm also single. I guess that's important."

"I'm going to make mad, passionate love to you." And with that, Desifinado leaned across the table, causing it to tip severely, spilling our drinks.

I jumped nervously to my feet. "Let me get some napkins."

While wiping up our mess, I fantasized about Desi carrying me into his large, virile bedroom, and laying me down on his overstuffed pillows neatly piled in rows on his queen-size mahogany sleigh bed, which would be decked out in coordinated Martha Stewart sheets from K-Mart. He leans over me, and then, ever so gently, we make contact. Mouth to mouth, lips to lips, breath to breath. Dizzy with thoughts of Desi ravaging me, I had to put my head between my knees to avoid fainting.

He knocked on the table. "Anybody home?"

"Just putting the napkins under the foot of the table to keep it from wobbling." *Breathe, Curtis, breathe.*

As I came back up, Desi planted his mouth on mine. Not gently or sensually. Our mouths did not lightly meet. There was no tender parting of lips or breath to breath. His tongue was already down my throat and heading for my pancreas. He was holding the back of my head so I couldn't pull away. Eventually he had to come up for air, but not before cutting my mouth with his darting tongue.

"Desi!" I yelped, pulling my face away from his.

He looked around to make sure people were watching. "It's your fault, Curt. You made me do it!"

"I made you do what?"

"I want to bathe you."

Caught off guard, I immediately pictured Desi bathing me. I'm coming home from a long, tiring day. A trail of rose petals leads me to the Jacuzzi in his master bath. A bottle of Veuve Clicquot is chilling in the sink. Candles are lit, and my bath is drawn. Clad only in a thong, Desifinado silently undresses me, lifts me up, kisses me passionately without any plunging tongue, and then slips me into the tub. He then bathes me from head to toe while I sip my favorite champagne. What can I say? I'm an incurable romantic.

He grabbed my hand and dragged me out of The Dixie Cup.

I had to get more information out of this guy. "So, tell me, Desi, what do you do for a living?"

"I'm very low-key about my careers."

"Careers? You sound like a real Renaissance man."

"I am."

And he's modest, too. He looked around to see if anyone was within hearing distance and then projected, as if he were in a twenty-five-thousand-seat stadium trying to reach the last row, "I'm on two soap operas at the same time."

"Two?" I whispered.

"*One Life to Live* and *Guiding Light*. I'm a contract player on both."

"Both?" I asked incredulously.

"Yes. It's very rare."

Is this a warning sign? Stop being so cynical, Curtis. Give him the benefit of the doubt.

"So what's it like to work with Kate Summers?"

"Who?"

"Kate Summers, the star of *Guiding Light?*"

"Oh, I don't know her. She's not in my storyline. I only read the parts of scripts that involve my story line."

One benefit of the doubt gone, two more to go.

Suddenly, Desi yelled out, "Lucy!"

A top-heavy bodybuilder with stick legs wearing a spaghetti-strap tank top and hot pants sashayed toward us. Didn't anyone tell him that spandex is carcinogenic?

"Lucy? It's Louie!" he screamed as they kissed the air on either side of their cheeks. "Dizzy, right?"

"Desi."

Desi and Lucy.

Louie looked at me out of the corner of his eye. "And who's your little friend?"

"This is Curt. We've been working out together for twelve years and this is our first date."

"What does a lesbian bring on the second date?" asked Louie. "A U-Haul. What does a gay man bring on the second date?"

"What second date?" Desi and Louie shouted out together.

"Enjoy it while it lasts, Gert."

"It's Curt. I mean, Curtis."

"Don't be a stranger, Desi." Then, looking at me, he said, "Call me like you said you would after we had *our* first date." And off Louie cackled.

Desi and I walked on in silence. Just then, he squeezed my hand and whispered, "Here we are."

We were standing on the corner of Sixth Avenue and 18th Street. I felt my heart racing; my pulse was pounding because this man, Desifinado, who speaks seven languages, has contracts on two different soap operas, and unself-consciously checks the back of his head with a woman's compact mirror in a men's locker room, was going to ask me up to his luxurious apartment, or maybe loft, bathe me, and then devour my body.

Desi headed for the door of the store on the ground floor. "Come with me."

"Into this store?" I asked while looking up at the sign.

"Yes, watch me buy an iron."

I wasn't sure I heard correctly. "A what?"

"I need an iron. I have an important engagement tonight, and I need an iron."

That was it. I put my foot down. "Desi? I would love to watch you buy an iron, but I do need to run." *See how strong I can be?*

"I miss you already. Give me your number," he ordered rather forcefully.

Reluctantly, I slipped him my card as he slipped me his tongue. But this time the kiss was more gentle and less drilling. It was almost passionate, almost sensitive, almost wanting, and I was almost melting 'cause he was on the right track.

He pulled away and said, "I'm busy for the next week. I'll call you when my schedule opens up."

And with that, he disappeared into *Bed, Bath & Begone!*

Dazed, to say the least, I walked a couple of blocks south when I meant to go north and then realized I was mad. I felt manipulated and played with and dissected, and how dare he say, "I'll call you when my schedule opens up." *The nerve. How dare he play with me like that?*

≥ ≤

Three days later and after taping each episode of both *One Life To Live* and *Guiding Light* and seeing neither hide nor hair of my dueling actor, I called Quinn in Los Angeles.

"Hi, it's me."

"Hey, Sweetie." Quinn ran out of the producer's booth on the set of *General Hospital* and into a stairwell. "I can only talk a second. They're taping one of my shows today."

"How's it going?"

Quinn brushed the sweat away from his brow. "I desperately want to give one actor, Cash Grant, a fucking line reading, but I'm being good."

I laughed at the name Cash Grant but was careful not to make fun of the soap industry. I had made that mistake one too many times with Quinn. The rules were that he had the right to criticize and joke about it, but I didn't. And I totally agreed. I hesitated for a second before explaining why I had called.

"Quinn, I met someone."

"Married and out of state?"

I started to rewind the tape of the soap operas, thinking

maybe I had missed him. "No, single and New York City."

Quinn dropped his cell and started cursing as he chased it down one flight of stairs. He picked it up, making sure that it still worked. He gasped. "Congrats. I'm going to faint."

"Tell me quickly, when you wrote for *One Life To Live,* do you remember an actor named Desi?"

He tapped his cell, thinking there was something wrong with it. "Dizzy?"

I pronounced his full name very deliberately. "Desifinado." I could hear his brain clicking.

"What's his last name?"

"One name, and it's Desifinado, like—"

"Charo?"

I knew there was a reason he was my best friend. "Yes, doesn't he sound Cuban?"

Quinn started back up the stairs. "He sounds stupid. There's a new doctor playing opposite Nina. Network loves him, but producers of the show think he reads too light."

I stopped the videotape to study the credits. "He says he's been on the shows awhile."

Quinn did a double take. "Shows?"

I was embarrassed that the tone that came out of my mouth was slightly proud. "Contracts with both *Guiding Light* and *One Life To Live.*" There was dead silence on Quinn's end. "Is that possible?"

"Very impossible, Curtis." At that moment, Cash Grant opened the stairwell door and headed toward Quinn. "He might be a contract player on one show or the other, but contractually, he can't be signed to two shows at once."

Quinn reached out for Cash, who passed without even acknowledging him. "Wait!" Quinn yelled. "I need to talk to you."

Cash turned around and reprimanded him. "Fans shouldn't be in this part of the building."

"Fans?" Quinn jumped out of his skin as Cash flew down the stairs. "I'm your fucking writer."

I turned off the VCR and threw the remote at it. "An out-of-work actor. I had a feeling Desi was full of bullshit."

Quinn had to address the actor. "Curtis, trust your instincts; they're always right. But at the same time, give him the benefit of the doubt. Got to run." He flew down the stairs after Cash, cursing at the top of his lungs.

I thought to myself, *Benefit of the doubt number two, Desi.*

≥ ≤

That night, at about eleven, I got not a phone call but a buzz from the intercom in my apartment. Startled, I answered the house phone.

"Yes?"

The voice was terribly garbled. "It's me."

"Me who?" I asked.

"You've forgotten already? Desi."

I didn't know what to say.

"Buzz me in. I'm coming up."

How dare he? How rude and pompous. Just showing up on my doorstep unannounced and so late at night. How does he know that I don't already have some hunk waiting for me in my bed? Does he think I'm going to drop everything for him? Does he think I'm so smitten with him that I'm just going to instantly buzz him in?

I buzzed him in.

By the time he rang my doorbell, I had had time to brush my teeth, wash my face, apply a moisturizer, make my bed, put dishes away, balance my checkbook, and pop a breath mint into my mouth. I live on a very high floor with a slow elevator.

I opened my front door and he pulled me into his arms, but not before I caught a glimpse of the side of his head. Was that a snap that I saw? Could he be wearing additional hair that snaps to his scalp? Distractingly, his mouth searched for mine. He was no longer tonguing or darting or even kissing. He was hovering with our lips barely touching. He had discovered my weakness.

Suddenly, he whizzed into my apartment. He handed me his coat and started taking his clothes off.

"Excuse me?" I said.

His shirt was up over his head. "I want us to nap together."

"Desi, it's eleven p.m. It's bedtime."

He kicked off his shoes. "I won't sleep with you on the second date."

"This is a date? You've shown up unannounced at my door."

"And you let me in." He dropped his pants. "I want you to strip down to your underwear. I need to discuss some important things with you, but no sex. Sex is too easy."

That's easy for him to say. I watched him bend over to pull off his socks and I got a good look at the top of his head. The hair was thinning, as if it was his, but the hairline itself seemed much too dark and too thick. What the hell was going on with his head?

"I didn't think you'd have such a nice apartment," Desi said, glancing around. "How can you afford this?"

I ignored his remarks. I can afford my apartment because it's a rental that I've lived in for almost twenty years. I couldn't afford it if it were at market value. My two-bedroom, two-and-a-half-bath was currently valued at $5,000 a month. Often I wondered what the new tenants in my building did for a living.

Desi continued with the backhanded compliments. "And it's so large, with a dining room and eat-in kitchen. The décor's neither modern nor traditional."

"I call it 'eclectic.' "

"I call it too busy, with too many colors. Where's your bedroom?" he asked as he went down my hallway.

I felt like asking him which bedroom, just to rub it in, but I held my tongue.

He found my bedroom and jumped onto my bed, motioning for me to join him. I pulled off my T-shirt and warm-up pants and sat upright on the side of the bed. He pushed me down into a prone position and wrapped his arms around me as I lay there like bullet man. I was tense, nervous, and fascinated.

"My father is a millionaire. He left my mother and now lives in Argentina."

"So you're Argentinean?"

"No. Shush."

I turned onto my side and started playing with a big lock of his hair. I was surprised that he didn't seem to notice.

He continued. "My father made millions in shoes. When I was a child, we lived on the Upper East Side."

"So, you're a native New Yorker?"

"Please don't talk. Shoes, who would've thought?"

Desi's hair felt brittle and dry.

"He had rinky-dink shoe stores strewn all across Long Island. I'm an only child and my mother's favorite."

"You're her only child?"

I started to twirl his hair.

"Are you going to listen or keep interrupting?"

"Sorry."

"My father kept it a secret that he was a millionaire. He made my mother and I work and struggle. I had a part-time job in high school, and one year I needed a pair of shoes."

"Of all things?" I added, twirling his hair harder and harder.

He stared me down. "I worked at the Rose Briar Country Club in northern New Jersey as a caddie, and by the end of the summer, I had saved up enough money to pay for my very own thirty-five-dollar pair of Keds sneakers."

He turned away, and I was horrified to see that the hair I was playing with had fallen out of his head.

Desi was quiet. I looked over at him and he was crying. I really didn't mean to hurt him.

"Desi, I'm so sorry. I had no idea."

He turned back to me. "I knew you'd feel bad that I had to buy my own pair of shoes."

He hadn't felt a thing. He didn't know I had yanked out his hair. I quickly threw it on the floor.

He bolted upright. "There's someone in this room," Desi declared while sniffing the air.

"It's just you and me."

His eyes searched the room. "No, I'm psychic. There's someone here. A depressed soul."

I laughed. "Is it dead or alive?"

"I'd better get going."

Desi ran out of the bedroom, down the hallway, through my dining room, and into the front hall, where he jumped into his pants.

"Curt, we'll have to cleanse your apartment with burning sage on my next visit." He threw on his shirt. "I love the way we share." He stepped into his shoes and grabbed his coat. He gave me a big bear hug and said, "I'll let you know when you can see me again."

And then he left.

Fuck you, Desi. Fuck you for playing with me again.

I wonder when he'll call?

≷ ≷

While riveted to *The Operation* show on television, which was showing a man having the back of his scalp slit open and then pulled up and over the top of his head to solve his premature balding, my phone rang.

"Hello?"

"You miss me?"

I had to play hard to get. "No."

"Come down to Bryant Park."

I can be strong. "No, thank you."

"I'm joining a few friends for a free jazz concert. You must come and meet them."

I can be aloof. "Nope, I'm busy."

"Three o'clock sharp. Can't wait to share with you. Ciao."

≳ ≲

I showed up ten minutes early.

The jazz festival, if that's what you could call it, had already started. What these musicians lacked in talent they made up for in volume.

It was an absolutely perfect Saturday afternoon, which may have explained why so many people had shown up. Located directly behind the New York Public Library, Bryant Park is a small but charming oasis open to residents, workers, and tourists alike. Today it was packed with all types of people, ranging from toddlers to octogenarians, bag people to corporate CEOs.

For at least thirty minutes, I lugged the heaviest bag full of goodies around, searching the lawn for Desifinado. We New Yorkers are pack mules.

Having no luck, I was about to give up and head back uptown when he appeared. He wasn't carrying anything.

"Sorry I'm late!" he shouted while waving to me.

I was angry with him but angrier with myself. But did I show it?

"Don't worry, Desi. You're on time. I was early. I just can't believe I came."

"I knew you would."

I knew he knew I would. We stood face-to-face. He looked so incredibly handsome, and he was fully aware of it. He stretched out his arms, embraced me warmly, and whispered the lyrics of the song that was being played at that moment into my ear. *You'd be so easy to love, Desi,* I thought to myself.

My knees buckled, and as he caught me, I gave his skull the third degree, searching for signs of scalp-reconfiguration scars.

I pulled a blanket out of my tote bag as he gestured to an open area.

"Let's set up over here, Curt. Did you bring anything to eat?"

I pointed to the bag. "Not really. Just some vegetable pâté, water crackers, grilled vegetables, marinated chicken breasts, couscous, and a bottle of wine." I held it out to him.

He looked at the label, frowned, and then pretentiously said, "Not a very good year."

A voice inside of me said *Leave now,* so I sat down. I handed him a corkscrew, and he opened the wine as a singer joined the so-called musicians and warbled through his rendition of "I Fall In Love Too Easily." How appropriate.

"So, who else is coming?" I asked as I pulled out two wine-glasses.

"Akmar, the nineteen-year-old exiled crown prince of Iran, who is my new best friend, and who has invited me to stay with him at his temporary palace in Croatia whenever I want, met my old best friend Hunter online. They've been having a torrid love affair for the past two weeks. However, Hunter met a man at the Diesel Bar on Christopher Street last night and told Akmar that he won't be back until six thirty tomorrow morning, and this enraged the prince so much that he has left early and returned to his homeland. Sorry, it's just you and me, kid."

I set out two china plates as he poured the wine. "I don't mind."

He moved a little closer to me. "Curt, is there anything you feel compelled to tell me?"

I pulled away. "Yes, I feel compelled to ask you to stop asking that question."

Just then, Desi looked beyond me to someone and shouted, "Do you know Keith Hernandez?"

I turned around and saw a woman wearing a Keith Hernandez baseball shirt while breast-feeding a huge child. She pulled the kid off of her nipple, leaving her areola exposed. "No, I don't know Keith, I'm just a big fan."

"I'm Keith's hands," Desi declared.

Both the woman and I asked, "What?"

"I'm Keith Hernandez's hands in a toilet-paper commercial. I'm a hand model, and I have perfect hands."

I can't believe I'm on a date with a man who's a hand model and proud *of it.*

As everyone on the lawn looked over due to the fact that Desi had announced this so that it could be heard over the annoying music, he stood up and raised his precious and important hands up into the air, like a doctor after having scrubbed and prepped for surgery.

Like a human bullhorn, he announced to all of Bryant Park, "I have Keith Hernandez's hands."

"Too bad you don't have his bank account," I rejoiced.

A roar of laughter erupted from the crowd. I just couldn't resist, and I toasted them with my glass of wine.

Embarrassed, Desi sat back down on the blanket.

After a moment, he said in a very dramatic voice, "Well, give him some cheap wine and an audience and he turns evil."

I removed two white cloth napkins and refolded them, placing them on our plates. "What was that?" I asked, knowing perfectly well what he had said.

"I had no idea you were a comedian," he hissed.

I dug my hand into my bag and emerged with a scented candle.

"I'm not. But if you had asked me, I would have told you what I do. In fact, you haven't asked me one question about me."

I searched the bag for matches, but there were none to be found. How was I going to light the candle? Maybe I could ask Desi to just breathe on it.

"That's a lie, Curt. I asked you several times if there was anything you felt compelled to tell me."

"*Too* many times. And that's not asking me something about me, or what I like to do in my spare time, or how many siblings I have, or what kind of music I listen to, or what I think of breast-feeding in public."

"I can see you're high-maintenance."

I finally had a good idea. "I'm outta here." I threw the silverware back into the bag.

He desperately tried defending her to me. "Breast-feeding is a very natural thing."

"Yes, I know it's natural, Desi. What's not natural is that she's doing it exhibitionist-style at a jazz concert with a captive audience. She's getting off on it." I grabbed the napkins and threw them in.

"It's a very common thing in Europe. To breast-feed your child in public."

I put the candle back in the bag.

"Well, we're not in Europe, and what she's doing is probably illegal. That kid is old enough to ask for it."

He curled his upper lip and looked at me with utter disdain. "You Americans."

"Desi, where were you born?"

"The Bronx. Why?"

I shrugged my shoulders and stood with the two wineglasses. "Never mind."

"You're too sensitive and so quick to judge." He patted the blanket next to him. "Please, relax and come to my side. What do you feel compelled to tell me, Curt?"

Holding back the rage I was beginning to feel, I emptied out the wineglasses and managed to say, "Desi, I'm a very honest and up-front kind of guy. I feel compelled to tell you—"

And suddenly he pulled me down, grasped my head, and began sucking on my ear. Not nibbling. Not kissing. Nursing on my earlobe. And just before I could pull away, he whispered, "I'm still in love with my ex-lover."

I broke away from his suction, wineglasses still in hand. "You're what?"

"We were together for three years. We broke up earlier this year, and he's moved to Chicago. I'm up-front and honest, too. I'm still in love with him."

I looked at him in shock. "But you said you were single again and that I'd be so easy to love."

"And you would be. But Antoine is still in my heart. You can't erase history."

"So why are we doing all of this?"

"Because it was meant to be. Because you are so handsome. Because you made me do it."

I stood up again. "I didn't make you do anything. Desi, let's just call it a day."

"What are you saying?"

"I'm not going to start anything with someone who blatantly tells me he's in love with his ex."

"Why are you doing this to me?"

With that, he started cry.

"Desi, there's no reason to take this so hard."

"Curt, I haven't felt this much emotion, this much connection, this much feeling for another man in at least a month."

A month?

"Curt, please don't shut me out yet. I'll be more attentive. I'll be more of whatever you need. I'm really a very loving and compassionate person. There isn't a fake bone in my body. I'm the real thing."

61

"Oh, really? Well, here's what I feel compelled to tell you, Desi. I'm HIV-positive."

He stopped crying.

"I have been for over sixteen years, at the least. But never sick, thank God."

Desi looked as though he had seen a ghost. He literally turned pale and started to shake.

"But you kissed me."

"No, Desi, you kissed me. And thanks for the compassion."

"How could you let me do that?"

This guy was fucking unbelievable. "Excuse me? You ambushed my mouth on each occasion."

He sat back down on the blanket. "Okay, you'll just have to fill me in on the intricacies of having sex with someone who is positive."

I dropped to my knees in front of him, exasperated. "The intricacies of having sex with someone who is positive? Desi, you should be having the same type of sex with me that you have with all the guys who tell you they are negative. Safe sex."

"But I've never been with someone who is positive."

"You've never been with someone who *told* you he was positive. Trust me. There are plenty of guys out there who are lying. I just happen to tell the truth."

"But I kissed you." He wiped his lips. "Am I at risk?"

"Yes, you're at risk for me bashing your face in. You can't get HIV from kissing. What century are you living in?"

And then he said it, the one obvious but idiotic phrase that infuriates me. "I'm negative, and I plan on staying that way. I think we have a problem."

I stood up. "We have a problem? You think we have a problem? Desifinado?"

"Yes, Curt?"

I started packing up everything. "Three benefits of the doubt.

You're out. It's been different. I'll go my way. You go yours. You are truly one of the most insensitive, self-centered, narcissistic liars I have ever met."

He stood up and put his face right into mine. "I resent that. I am not a liar."

I had been aching to call him on this. "You can not be contractually signed to two soap operas at the same time."

"So I padded my résumé."

"And your head."

"I beg your pardon?"

I shot a disgusted glance up to his hair. "I don't know what's going on north of your forehead, but it ain't real. You should just shave it; bald is in."

He patted his head gingerly. "Every hair on my head is real."

"It's definitely real." I tried to touch it, and he pulled away. "It's just not yours."

"This is so petty." He got to his feet. "I'm so disappointed in you."

I picked up a corner of the blanket and waited as he reluctantly moved. "The feeling's mutual, Desi. And when we pass each other in the gym, let's pretend none of this ever happened. We'll just acknowledge each other with a nod or a flick of the finger or a grunt. And if I don't talk to you for another twelve years, please don't take it personally."

I threw the blanket into the bag.

"Okay, Curt, if you're going to be that way. And next time? Tell a guy up front and right away that you are positive. Have a good life."

"Yeah, you too, Desi."

As I walked away, he very dramatically shouted to me, "You're missing out on a really classy guy, Curtis."

I couldn't believe the jerk finally said my name correctly. I turned back, trying to think of some clever retort, when the jazz combo started playing what sounded vaguely like "Stormy Weather."

A gust of wind whipped through the crowd, lifting the back flap of Desi's hair, and suddenly I remembered what he had said to me. If you want something badly, with all your heart, the universe will conspire to make it happen. And that's when the powers that be answered my prayer.

Like a champagne cork popping out of a bottle, the wind caught hold of that thing on top of his head and—whether it was glued on, sutured, plugged in, or snapped on—off it went, sailing up into the sky.

In his desperate attempt to save his dignity and his flying carpet, Desi tripped over my cheap, "not a good year" bottle of wine, which sent him hurtling to the ground, grinding his palms into a bed of gravel.

"My hands!" he screamed. He held them up, but this time they were bleeding. "My perfect hands are ruined. I'm ruined!"

I smiled to myself, thinking that there is a God, after all.

FIVE

ENTRAPMENT

I'm a speed typist, and proud of it. I've won awards. Well, back in junior high, that is. It was mandatory for us to take typing class, for which I am so grateful now. Miss Huggnutz (yes, that was her name) was our typing teacher. She was poised, smartly dressed, not unlike an airline hostess, and more beautiful out of her clothes than in.

After she returned from a trip to Paris one summer, she insisted on sunbathing in her backyard in the nude. Lucky for us, Ernie Tisbit lived next door and took quite a collection of pictures of Miss Huggnutz. He charged each one of us fifty cents to look at them during lunchtime.

I remember my mother calling her "tres risqué." I couldn't find those words in our dictionary, so I just assumed that it referred to her private parts.

Needless to say, Miss Huggnutz was a great typing teacher. One technique she used to increase our accuracy and speed was to put on a record of Howard Johnson music. We would type to the rhythm, which would gradually increase in tempo.

At age fourteen, during my eighth-grade graduation ceremony, I was asked to come up onstage to receive my rather large plastic typewriter award for fastest typist in the school. I was capable of ninety words a minute with no errors on a manual. I was the definition of a nerd.

When I got my first electric typewriter, I was delighted.

When I got my first word processor, I was in heaven. When I got my first computer, I was panicked.

Somehow, the computer concept frightened me to death, and I resisted it until my mother started yelling at me because she couldn't send me e-mail. Her screen name is Dustyboots, by the way.

I just had to break down and switch over. So, it's no wonder that I was behind in accessing the Internet, not to mention chat rooms.

≳ ≲

MrStudMan:	<eg>
BUFFEDnNYC:	Name is Curtis. I'm kind of new to chatting, what does <eg> mean?
MrStudMan:	evil grin
BUFFEDnNYC:	<ei>
MrStudMan:	whatz that
BUFFEDnNYC:	EVIL EYE
MrStudMan:	lol
BUFFEDnNYC:	which means?
MrStudMan:	laughing out loud...u a (_o_)
BUFFEDnNYC:	Am I an asshole?
MrStudMan:	a bottom
BUFFEDnNYC:	I don't buy into this top/bottom thing. What happens...happens.
MrStudMan:	then ur a (_o_)
BUFFEDnNYC:	ROTFLOL
MrStudMan:	whatz that
BUFFEDnNYC:	ROLLING ON THE FLOOR LAUGHING OUT LOUD
MrStudMan:	k
BUFFEDnNYC:	So, you and I have been chatting long enough, want to trade?
MrStudMan:	trade what?

BUFFEDnNYC:	BASEBALL CARDS! You know exactly what I mean! Self-pics!
MrStudMan:	no pic
BUFFEDnNYC:	Why not? CVS will scan them now for $4.99.
MrStudMan:	not that...people keep sending it out...saying its them
BUFFEDnNYC:	Then you must be handsome.
MrStudMan:	no complaints yet
BUFFEDnNYC:	Well, I have no qualms about sending out my pic
MrStudMan:	whatz a qualm
BUFFEDnNYC:	Never mind. I'm sending it now.
MrStudMan:	k
BUFFEDnNYC:	YOU'VE GOT MAIL!
MrStudMan:	u r fast
BUFFEDnNYC:	No, my computer is. :-)
MrStudMan:	damn, u r hot...i want that... :^o)~
BUFFEDnNYC:	You want WHAT?!!!!!
MrStudMan:	that really u
BUFFEDnNYC:	YES! It's really me!!!!!!
MrStudMan:	meat me now
BUFFEDnNYC:	MEAT you? LOL! On my end, this is a blind connection!
MrStudMan:	u want to travel?
BUFFEDnNYC:	Do you mean do I want to come to you?
MrStudMan:	my apartment
BUFFEDnNYC:	I think if we meet, it's in a public place first
MrStudMan:	k...but i want sum of that
BUFFEDnNYC:	We're both on the upper west side...how about The Sinners...that new bar on 109th and Amsterdam? Curtis here.
MrStudMan:	carl...kewl...leaving now
BUFFEDnNYC:	WAIT! How will I recognize you?
MrStudMan:	i'll recognize u...see u in 15...ciao
BUFFEDnNYC:	But...

⋝ ⋜

But MrStudMan had already signed off. The Internet and online chatting had created the electronic bar of the new millennium. Meeting people like this was a little too fast, a little too easy, a little too addictive...and I was hooked.

So I threw on a pair of blue jeans and a white T-shirt and dashed out the door. Unfortunately, I didn't know it was raining. I decided against wasting time going back upstairs to my apartment for an umbrella and ran out to Amsterdam Avenue to hail a cab. Of course, there were none in sight.

I ended up walking the nineteen blocks, which gave me more than enough time to reflect upon my first Internet "connection." He had been vertically challenged, to say the least.

⋝ ⋜

BUFFEDnNYC:	You have a very nice face.
TALLnHNDSM:	u like tall guys?
BUFFEDnNYC:	I'm not really into height. I mean, tall, medium, short. It's not an issue with me. I'm more interested in meeting a guy with a smart mind and an open heart.
TALLnHNDSM:	cuz im 6'5"
BUFFEDnNYC:	Wow! That is tall.
TALLnHNDSM:	tall enuf 4 u?
BUFFEDnNYC:	Maybe too tall!
TALLnHNDSM:	what?
BUFFEDnNYC:	just kidding

≳ ≴

I decided to meet this very tall and handsome man at a bar. He had arrived early and had perched himself on a stool. And I mean perched. What first caught my attention was the fact that he seemed to have a rather short torso for someone who is 6'5".

I looked a little closer and saw that his legs were dangling from the chair, light years away from the floor. I gently slid in next to him at the bar and introduced myself, noticing that he had almost finished a beer.

We exchanged hellos and chatted for a while, but it was obvious to both of us that things weren't clicking. After I finished my first beer and he finished his second, we decided to go our separate ways.

But I was determined to see how tall he was; therefore, I went on and on, talking about nothing till he finally said he had to hit the men's room. He jumped off of the barstool and tiptoed off to the bathroom.

When he came back, he stood right in front of me as I looked down at him.

"What gives?" I asked him.

He wouldn't look me in the eye. "If I had told you that I was four-ten you wouldn't have wanted to meet me," he said in his tallest voice.

I bent down so we were face-to-face. "Like I said, I have no issues with height. But I do have issues with liars. How did you think you were going to get away with this?"

"I knew you wouldn't like me, so I knew I wouldn't have to get off of the barstool."

Talk about low self-esteem. "Let me give you a little bit of advice. If you're going to lie about something"—and then I looked right at his crotch—"lie about something I can't see."

≳ ≲

The rain had shifted from a sexy mist to a heavy downpour. I entered The Sinners ten minutes late and looking like a drowned rat.

I headed straight for the bathroom. However, on route, a man I had dated—not briefly enough, thank you very much—spotted me.

"Curtis!" he hollered.

I stopped dead in my tracks and turned to look at him.

"You never returned my last phone call," he chided me.

"Hello, George."

George is truly one of the most boring people I have ever met in my entire life. Plus, he's a whiner.

"I've called you at least six times, and you haven't returned any of my messages."

He also doesn't get a hint.

"George, I'm kinda in a rush, and, as you can see, I'm soaking wet, and now I'm standing in front of an air conditioner. This isn't a good time."

"That's your problem," he informed me. "You never have time. You never have time for me. You only have time for you." He started jabbing his index finger into my chest. "It's all about you, you, you."

"Yes, George, it's all about me." I pushed him aside. "Now, if you'll excuse me, I have to—"

"Curtis?" asked a voice from behind.

I turned around, and standing before me was MrStudMan. Let me just say, that's exactly what he was.

"Mr. Stud." I laughed nervously. "I mean, Carl?"

"In the flesh." He spread his legs and crossed his arms. "So, you like?"

I had to blurt it out: "I like."

I took Carl by the arm and dragged him to the front of the bar where there was lounge seating.

"Curtis, I'm going to call you," threatened George, "and I expect you to at least have the decency to return it."

I laughed him off and pushed Carl into a love seat. "Here, sit. Stay. Sit, Carl, sit. What can I get you?"

"Corona?"

"With a lime?"

He nodded. Let me just fill you in. Carl was 6'1" and two hundred pounds of solid muscle. He had this mane of copper-colored hair, piercing blue eyes, and a mustache. He looks just like the Marlboro Man. *Inhale, Curtis, inhale.*

Armed with two Coronas, I sat next to Carl. Damn, he even smelled good, like fresh laundry. "So, have you met many guys online?" I asked, thinking to myself what a stupid question that was.

"No, I just recently went online."

A red flag went up, but I ignored it, because Carl was *gorgeous.*

"I see. I've met quite a few. I mean, I've met a few but not quite a few. Well, I don't mean a lot. I've met some that have been mostly disaster stories. But I don't want you to get the idea that I'm some sort of cyber-slut or anything. I've, well, I've met…a few," I confessed as Carl looked deeply into my eyes with those ice-blue babies of his.

Just take your time, Curtis. Don't blow it. Don't rush it. This guy's a catch. No knee-jerk decisions.

"Want to go to my place?" he asked.

"Yes."

≥ ≤

It was still raining hard, but Carl had an umbrella and lived just three blocks from the bar. After climbing the five flights to his one-bedroom tenement, I nervously asked if I could use the bathroom.

"Sure," he said. "Want another beer?"

"Okay," I said as I shut the bathroom door.

I splashed cold water on my face and looked into the mirror.

What are you doing, kiddo? Taking a chance on—and the next words just didn't come out naturally—*love? Yeah, right.*

As I toweled off my face, I could hear Carl on the phone. And, believe me, it's not that I was eavesdropping; I could just hear him.

"I know I said ten but it's nine thirty now. Can we push it to ten thirty?"

There was a pause, and I wasn't breathing. He continued.

"Of course I do…You're hot; I want some of that…I'll be finished here in thirty minutes max, and then I'm all yours. Okay?" He hung up the phone.

I couldn't make it to the door fast enough.

"Hey, man, whaddaya doing?"

"Leaving."

He blocked the door. "Why?"

"I heard the phone conversation!"

I tried to squeeze my way by him, but he wouldn't budge. "Oh, that? That's just my brother. Haven't seen him in ages. He wants to catch up."

"Into incest? I'm out of here."

I pushed him out of the way and flew out the door.

He yelled down the hall to me as I ran down the stairs: "Asshole!"

I felt horrible. I walked home slowly in the heavy rain, letting the water cleanse me of the ugly scenario in which I had almost played a part.

Recognizing that the best thing for me to do would be to just crawl into bed and sleep it off, I chose to go back online.

I had to use a different screen name, of course. BUFFEDnNYC had to be put away for a while. I had to bring out a new persona, one that was unique, one that shouted out "brains and sense of humor." I decided on MUSCLEnNY.

I was online no more then two minutes when I got an instant message from none other than...MrStudMan.

≳ ≲

MrStudMan:	like ur screen name
MUSCLEnNY:	thnx
	(Notice I'm not only a new identity but also a new style of writing, too.)
MrStudMan:	lQQkin 2 hook up
MUSCLEnNY:	maybe...like ur profile...bet u have no problem meeting hot guys
MrStudMan:	nope
MUSCLEnNY:	bet u even hook up with 2 maybe 3 in a day
MrStudMan:	would that turn u on
MUSCLEnNY:	maybe
MrStudMan:	I fucked a guy at 6pm and fucked another one just now
MUSCLEnNY:	u r hungry
MrStudMan:	and in between i met a guy at the sinners and he came over
MUSCLEnNY:	tell me about the first guy
MrStudMan:	hot...not beautiful...but nice azz
MUSCLEnNY:	and the last guy?
MrStudMan:	attractive...hot...and big dik

MUSCLEnNY:	and what about the middle guy?
MrStudMan:	he was the FUCKING best
MUSCLEnNY:	FUCKING?
MrStudMan:	yeah, a writer but has the most incredible body
MUSCLEnNY:	so, what happened with him?
MrStudMan:	I FUCKED him
MUSCLEnNY:	YOU WHAT????!!!!!!
MrStudMan:	yeah, great azz and hung too
MUSCLEnNY:	OH REALLY? How big?
MrStudMan:	almost ten
MUSCLEnNY:	wow and he was a (_o_)?
MrStudMan:	yep and a fem
MUSCLEnNY:	A WHAT!!!????
MrStudMan:	u know...he was fem
MUSCLEnNY:	NO I DON'T KNOW! YOU MEAN HE HAD A LIMP WRIST AND TALKED WITH A LISP?????
MrStudMan:	u r funny
MUSCLEnNY:	WHAT MADE HIM FEM?
MrStudMan:	he started crying while I was fucking him
MUSCLEnNY:	I WHAT????!!!!
MrStudMan:	u?
MUSCLEnNY:	I mean him, why did he start crying?
MrStudMan:	guess I was too big
MUSCLEnNY:	or maybe you're just not a great top and you were hurting him
MrStudMan:	no, couldn't do that...he was like the lincoln tunnel
MUSCLEnNY:	WHAT!!!!????
MrStudMan:	and too emotional...looking at me with "be my lover" eyes
MUSCLEnNY:	man, don't you just hate that
MrStudMan:	u sound kewl and hot...want 2 hook up
MUSCLEnNY:	more than u know
MrStudMan:	company or travel

MUSCLEnNY:	company
MrStudMan:	nice profile...what ur stats
MUSCLEnNY:	5'9,"165, brown hair, hazel eyes, lean, cut, ripped muscle boy, 8 cut versatile
MrStudMan:	what u into...im vanilla to kink. (Vanilla to kink!?)
MUSCLEnNY:	same here
MrStudMan:	give me address (Now let me think. Carl lives up on 112th Street and Broadway. Let's send him to the farthest part of town. How about...?)
MUSCLEnNY:	525 East 3rd St. Apt 2F as in FUCK
MrStudMan:	Man, that's far...don't have enuf cash
MUSCLEnNY:	if ur worth it, I'll pay for ur cab
MrStudMan:	i'm worth it
MUSCLEnNY:	good...then get your ass over here now
MrStudMan:	signing off

≳ ≲

And he did. Mission accomplished. Entrapment! Life is beautiful. Basking in my own cleverness, I imagined Carl jumping into a cab and going all the way down to Alphabet City, which was going to cost him at least twentybucks, and he'd get no answer from the buzzer at 2F. That is, if there *was* a 2F. Or, for that matter, if there's even a building at 525 East 3rd Street. He'd have to ditch the cab driver, who would hopefully try to run him over, and then how would poor Carl get all the way back to the Upper West Side? He was stupid enough not to ask for my phone number.

How dare he say that he had had sex with me? I was flattered that he liked my body and thought that I had a big dick, but I am not the Lincoln Tunnel. And I am definitely not fem. I'm always careful about speaking in my lower register and not using too many hand movements when I talk. And what's this about me making "be my lover" eyes? Man, was *he* fucked up.

I know what you're thinking now. *It's bad karma*, Curtis. Well, you're right. But it was bad Karma for Carl to do what he did to me. What happened to him was cosmic retribution. I'm clear.

Knowing that I had done the world a good turn, I decided to relax and do something productive, so I got back online.

I did a search for the kind of guy I'm looking for. I entered: gay, masculine, single, theater, film, travel, cooking, gardening, relationship-oriented, and hung. And out of all the people registered with profiles online, only one name popped up, and he was actually online. It was fate.

≥ ≤

MUSCLEnNY:	Hey guy! Nice profile. I did a search and you're the ONE!
UNmeLOVERS:	thnx
MUSCLEnNY:	what's up?
UNmeLOVERS:	just got in
MUSCLEnNY:	me too
UNmeLOVERS:	like your profile too. You sound hot and nice. What do you do?
MUSCLEnNY:	writer...plays, books...some screenplays optioned
UNmeLOVERS:	kewl...name?
MUSCLEnNY:	Curtis...and yours?
	(Long pause.)
MUSCLEnNY:	still there?
UNmeLOVERS:	yep...just reading your profile again...so nice...
MUSCLEnNY:	want to trade?
UNmeLOVERS:	new to online...no pic yet...stats are accurate and would love to see yours...<g>

MUSCLEnNY: no problem...you seem like a good guy...sending

UNmeLOVERS: I am one of the good guys...WOW...you are handsome and have a great body.

MUSCLEnNY: <<blushing>> we have a lot of similar hobbies...do you meet guys from online?

UNmeLOVERS: very seldom

MUSCLEnNY: OH...me too

UNmeLOVERS: but I'd really like to meet you...

MUSCLEnNY: REALLY!!!!!!????? :)

UNmeLOVERS: I've been trying to use AOL specifically as a tool to collide into my soul mate.

MUSCLEnNY: well, then, fasten your seat belt...LOL...we've just hit head-on!

UNmeLOVERS: when can we meet?

MUSCLEnNY: like I said, I very seldom do this...but how about... let's say...in 15 min? LOL

UNmeLOVERS: you up to meeting tonight?

MUSCLEnNY: sure...if you are

UNmeLOVERS: great! I was going to say there's a really romantic restaurant around the corner from me...but I think it's closed by now

MUSCLEnNY: do you want to throw caution to the wind and meet at either my place or yours?

UNmeLOVERS: well...okay...I feel like I can trust you...want to come over?

MUSCLEnNY: YES!!!!!!!!!!

UNmeLOVERS: but in light of how we're meeting...let's think of us as friends first and if there's chemistry... <eg>

MUSCLEnNY: I LOVE THE WAY YOU THINK!

UNmeLOVERS: where are you?

MUSCLEnNY: Upper West Side

UNmeLOVERS: I'm all the way downtown...Battery Park City

MUSCLEnNY: no problem...I'll just jump in a cab

UNmeLOVERS:	EXCELLENT...458 Battery Park City Building #10, Apt 11B
MUSCLEnNY:	I'm leaving now! LOL
UNmeLOVERS:	see ya
MUSCLEnNY:	BYE

I caught one. I caught myself a good one. Exhilarated, I jumped into a cab and practically flew down to the tip of Manhattan. Who cares that it cost just over twenty bucks? I knew my new lover was worth it.

The problem with Battery Park City is that it's like a maze in which the buildings aren't very clearly marked. As I was looking for building number 10, a security guard came up to me.

"What are you doing?" he asked suspiciously.

I tried to look over his shoulder at the next building's address. "Looking for number ten?"

"There is no building number ten."

I defied him. "Yes there is."

"Trust me, we only go up to eight," he informed me. "So you better move along."

Move along? What does he think I am, a street person? I'd better move along? Eventually, I moved along.

Later that night, after having spent just over twenty bucks to get back home, I wanted to go back online to give uNmeLOVERS a piece of my mind. Could you believe this guy? Wasting all that time and energy on such an immature thing as sending another person on a bogus goose chase? The nerve of that guy. So it was actually a surprise when I signed on and found a message waiting for me from him.

≥ ≤

FROM: uNmeLOVERS
TO: MUSCLEnNY
Curtis, If you had only returned my phone calls,
you would have discovered how great I really
am. Have a good life.

George
P.S. Don't call!

Touché, George.

SIX

RUNWAY

Did I dare walk by his window again, or should I cross the street? Passing by and flirting with the stylist positioned in the front window of the Hair Today, Gone Tomorrow salon was once a daily ritual. Now it had become an hourly obsession.

My first thought was that he must think I'm unemployed. Who else would have this much time on their hands? Or maybe he thinks I'm a delivery boy or, worse yet, a hooker. Whatever he thought, I had to go by his window just one more time.

Five minutes ago I had approached this man of my dreams head-on, walking southbound on Broadway. It was our first encounter of the day. My heart pounded as I saw him. An ebony hunk of a man, 6'3" of total grade-A beefcake.

It was eleven a.m.. He must have just gotten to work; he was sipping his coffee and looking out the window when our eyes met. As he lowered the mug (revealing all 258 of his perfectly straight, pearly-white teeth) and smiled at me, I tripped.

Having worn out my old sneakers from pacing back and forth in front of his shop, I had just put on a new pair of running shoes. The laces were too long and I had stepped on them. But it wasn't a total trip. I didn't fall and land flat on my face. Instead, I jerked forward, and in the most graceful manner, with flailing arms, rubber legs, and mild whiplash, I managed to stay upright. I looked over at him, immediately fearing a look of humor on his face. Instead, his expression was one of concern. I wanted him, but I had to keep walking.

I looped down and around 90th Street to waste some time before I headed back to smile again at my new lover. He'd probably be working on a client by then, so I had to be careful and discreet. I'll make a total fool out of myself, but it's him I didn't want to embarrass. Now, this route is tricky. It's a blind approach I'm making, kind of like landing at La Guardia.

I didn't want to look obvious, so I walked by the window and—in a nonchalant yet totally calculating way—I looked away and across the street just as I sensed he was about to see me. I kept walking, but I could feel his loving gaze. He wanted me to look at him. He wanted me to stop. He wanted me. Suddenly, I turned my head back, careful to keep my chin down because that's my sexy look, but not too far down, because that's my double-chin look. And then I brought my eyes up and he wasn't there.

Damn, where is he? I slowly walked up to his window and suddenly I heard, "Well, hello there." It was him, standing in the doorway of the salon. "We have to stop meeting like this," he said with a grin.

Frightened that our love affair was ending before it had even begun, I asked, "We do?"

"Yes. I've enjoyed your window-shopping, but now it's time for you to come inside and check out the merchandise."

I babbled some sort of gibberish as I tried to regroup and pull myself together.

"Come on in." He opened the shop door seductively. "My name is Calvin."

"Hi Calvin. My name is Curtis," I said, knowing that as I walked in I was going to throw up momentarily, that being my natural response to excitement. *I'm quick. I'm clever. Think fast, Curtis.*

"So, Calvin. I'd like to have a haircut."

He chuckled, a deep baritone laugh, and ran his hand over my recently sheared head. "There's not much to cut."

I giggled a little too high. "I forgot, I cut it myself yesterday with one of those home kits."

He skimmed his hands over my head and then squeezed the back of my neck, "And you did a beautiful job."

"Thanks. Well, I better get going."

Feeling like a total idiot, I headed for the door. Then Calvin grabbed my hand.

"But that doesn't mean I can't wash your hair for you."

I was melting. Calvin didn't have hands. He had mitts. No, he had big, manly mitts. He grabbed my clammy little palm with his warm, enveloping paw and pulled me to the back of the salon.

The two girls who wash hair were ordered by my Calvin to leave the room. They mumbled inaudibly to him as they left, obviously displeased at being displaced.

"So, Curtis, what do you do?" Calvin asked as he seated me in front of a sink. "Please tell me you're not a street hooker."

I couldn't believe he had said that. Speechless, I froze.

He massaged my contracted shoulders. "Relax, I know you're not."

My shoulders dropped.

"You're too old to be one."

My shoulders hiked back up, having been smacked in the face with reality. I cleared my throat. "Actually, I'm a writer."

Calvin turned on the water and asked, "Cool?"

"Yes, it is cool being a writer."

He hit the side of my head in an affectionately aggressive way that told me he was the boss. "No, I meant the water. Is it too cool?"

The water was cool, but I was getting warmer—a lot warmer.

Suddenly, Calvin squirted shampoo onto my head and began to wash my hair.

Throwing up may be my response to excitement, but deep relaxation is my response to someone washing my hair. For some people, meditation works, for others, it's Valium. For me, it's having my hair washed. And Calvin was good. He was truly making love to my scalp, massaging and stroking it. His long, strong fingers worked their way down my neck and up over my face. Unfortunately, Calvin was a little too good and I fell asleep.

He didn't wake me up. My snore did.

"Oh, did I fall asleep?"

"Yes," Calvin said with a grin. "But just for an instant. You sleep like an angel."

He threw a towel over my head and started rubbing my hair briskly.

"Would you like to have dinner?" he asked.

I pulled the towel off of my head.

"What? I'm not sure I heard you correctly."

"Would you like to have dinner?" he asked again.

I got out of the chair and followed him as we headed to the front of the shop. The way he strutted just reeked of testosterone. My legs felt like overcooked spaghetti. "I would love that."

"You free Friday night?"

"If I'm not, I will be," I said a little too eagerly.

"Great. Then how about we meet at Café Stefano at eight?"

"It's a date."

We stood at the front door, and I wondered whether I should pay for the shampoo.

As I reached into my pocket, he said, "Don't worry, it's on the house."

"Thank you, Calvin, but let me give you this," I said as I tried to hand him a tip.

"Keep it," he said. "There are other ways you can tip me."

And with a sexy grin, he opened the shop door and I left.

I was excited, to say the least. Calvin was a great dresser. He always looked classic. Never overstated. Never tacky. He was happening. So it's not surprising that it took me nearly two hours to figure out what to wear on this date.

Café Stefano was a chic gay restaurant for ten minutes. Then the bridge-and-tunnel straight crowd discovered it. Now it's mixed and comfortable.

I had chosen to wear a pair of black Dolce & Gabbana pants that look like they are painted on my body, a cobalt-blue Parke & Ronen top, and Prada belt and shoes. I was hip and broke. Although I knew nothing about the man, I was determined that he would be the one I was going to spend the rest of my life with. I knew Calvin would recognize my taste and my labels and know that my wardrobe was not made up of cheap International Male catalog items.

So I girded my loins and, knowing I hadn't overlooked any minor details, entered Café Stefano an unfashionably thirty minutes early.

But there was one major detail I had overlooked. Once inside the restaurant, I was bombarded by patrons yelling orders at me.

"More bread, sir!"

"We'd like our check!"

"My cosmopolitan isn't frozen!"

I stood frozen. They all thought I was a waiter. It's no wonder, because as I glanced around, I noticed that all the waiters were wearing cobalt-blue muscle shirts and tight black pants. I could have died. Unfortunately, I didn't.

I wormed my way through the overcrowded bar and managed to tell the bartender that I wanted a manhattan straight up with Maker's Mark. I may know nothing else in life, but I do know my bourbon.

In the thirty minutes it took for me to drink two manhat-

tans (on an empty stomach because I skipped lunch to keep my
stomach flat, even though I was famished), the bar cleared out
enough so that I could actually sit on a stool.

And then he arrived, my bald, goateed chunk of masculinity.

"Hey, girl!" Calvin squealed to the bartender. "Sister's
here."

"Runway!" shouted the bartender and all the waiters.

I fell off my stool.

Calvin spotted me on the floor. "There you are, my little
window-shopping prince," he lisped as he helped me up.

I didn't know which to address first. The fact that the whole
restaurant referred to him as "Runway" or how he was dressed.
He made the decision for me.

He gestured to my outfit. "You go, girl. I love what you're
wearing. International Male, like me?"

My heart sank, as did my large intestine. My reaction to
excitement may be throwing up and my reaction to having my
hair washed may be relaxation, but my reaction to horror is
diarrhea.

Calvin, or should I say Runway, was decked out in a white
polyester jumpsuit unzipped to his navel and platform shoes.
He wore a jacket-style mink coat over his huge shoulders, and
he was carrying a clutch under his arm. He looked like Mrs.
Shaft. I was mortified and glued to my seat for fear of having an
accident in my pants. What had happened to him?

"Like my wrap, Curtis? It was my Aunt Bessie's, and she was
just my size." He petted the dead rat. "I inherited most of her
clothes."

"Your coat is . . . different."

"Sure is baby. Just like your Runway." He turned to the
bartender. "Sweetie, get your little ole Runway a Coke and
vodka."

The bartender winked at him. "Coming right up, doll."

"Runway?" I asked.

He settled into his left hip. "Yes, baby?"

"What happened to Calvin?"

He shifted to his right hip. "Honey, that's just my real name. My friends call me Runway."

"As in landing strip?"

"No, as in model's ramp." Suddenly, he started sashaying down the bar. The entire restaurant applauded and shouted, "*Go* Runway! *Go* Runway! *Go* Runway!" as I shrank to the size of Kate Moss.

I ran for the door, but Runway was faster and got ahold of the back of my shirt. "Let's eat, Daddy."

He called me Daddy? That's like giving me a seat on the bus.

"Runway is starving, and I want to hear all about your little ole life." He motioned to the hostess to seat us.

I fumbled for a way out. "We could just have drinks and call it a night—"

"No way, sugar. Tonight we are together."

He grabbed what now felt like my very large, mittlike, masculine hand with his dainty, limp, over-cologned fingertips and dragged me to the table.

The hostess asked Runway if he'd like to check his coat, and he snapped back, "It's not a coat, it's a mink. And I'm not taking it off so someone can steal it."

The hostess and I looked at each other, both wondering who would want to steal the thing.

The waiter handed us menus.

"I don't order from menus," barked Runway. "I create my own dinners."

The waiter did a double take and then left.

Please come back, nice, normal waiter dressed in a cobalt-blue muscle shirt and black pants just like me. Please come back and be my lover for the rest of my life and don't leave me alone with Runway.

"So, boo, tell me all about yourself."

Runway smiled a toothy grin, and I noticed for the first time that his 258 pearly whites were all dental implants, and a little too large at that. I felt my bowels about to evacuate.

He babbled on about how he had zipped through the Queens School of Hair Styling and Cosmetology in a record six-and-a-half years and explained that it was important for him to maintain a butch, sexy, masculine persona for his clientele at work, but that in real life he's just "little ole Runway, the girl next door."

The waiter reappeared. "Have you decided?"

"Yes," I declared, eager to confess that this was not the man I was going to spend the rest of my life with. Or girl.

"I can see you're new here. My name is Runway and this is . . ." He looked at me blankly. "Baby doll . . . help me. I've—"

"It's Curtis."

"Yes, this is Curt."

Not again.

"And tonight I want something different. Something unusual. Something sophisticated. I think I'll have a filet mignon with a béarnaise sauce."

"But that's not on the menu," replied the waiter as I hid behind mine.

"I know it's not. I'm creating my own dinner, and I want filet mignon with a béarnaise sauce."

"Sir," the waiter said calmly, "we do have filet mignon, but this is a mediocre Italian restaurant with a new Mexican chef. I promise you, you won't be getting a béarnaise sauce."

"Fine, I'm not going to argue. Just bring me the filet mignon plain and a side of macaroni and cheese."

But I thought Calvin was sophisticated?

The waiter turned to me. "And you, sir?"

"I'll just have a Caesar salad?"

"What?" exclaimed Runway.

"I had a big lunch. I'm not very hungry."

The waiter started to leave.

"But I will have another manhattan straight up with Marker's Mark," I said desperately.

I don't remember much about dinner. And, trust me, it wasn't because of the manhattans. I was cold sober. I believe my lack of memory was instinctual self-preservation. Selective memory. However, I do remember Calvin—I'm sorry, Runway—saying at one point that he believed in love at first sight when he saw me through the window and that he'd had a breast reduction. He had also developed this white frothy foam in the corners of his mouth. This was the date from hell.

The next thing I remember, we were traveling uptown in a cab.

"You'll love this place," promised Runway.

"Where are we going?"

He dug into his clutch, pulled out a tube of mauve-colored lipstick, and proceeded to lather it on. "To the Noel Coward."

I had to object. "But that's a seedy old gay bar on the other side of town."

He pulled out a bottle of Passion perfume and told me that he had friends at the Noel Coward and assured me that it would be a fabulous adventure. He cocked his head away, attempted to spray his neck, and ending up getting me right in the eyes.

I let out a cry as the perfume seared my corneas.

"Besides, Curt, I've done all the talking tonight. Now I want to hear your story."

Adventure? My story? I just wanted to go home and never look through another window as long as I lived. Actually, if my eyes continued to swell and burn, I wouldn't be looking through much of anything except a mist of tears.

We arrived at the Noel Coward, and it was still a seedy old gay bar nobody would be caught dead in. Upon our entry, the entire place shouted, "Runway!"

I plopped myself down on a barstool and ordered a glass of water as Runway took off for the men's room.

Ten minutes later and worried, I went back toward the bathroom.

I heard giggling, whispering, and blowing of noses. I tried to enter but the door was locked, so I knocked.

Two voices answered, "Who is it?"

"Runway, are you in there?

"Yes, baby cakes. I'll be right out."

I sat back down at the bar.

After a total of twenty minutes of being in the bathroom, which gave me more than enough time to seethe with anger, Runway came up from behind and wrapped his arms around me. I slipped out of his hold and turned to him. It looked like he had been eating a sugar donut.

"What have you been doing?" I asked.

"Powdering my nose?" he replied, laughing, as he wiped the cocaine off with his finger and then massaged it into his gums.

I grabbed my coat and headed for the door.

"Sweet meat, this is your *Run* way."

"Don't call me sweet meat, and you are not mine."

He caught my elbow as I was just about to make my escape. Spinning me around, he tried to kiss me. I weaseled my way out of his grip, pulled away, and tried to stand up to his 6 feet, 3 inches.

"You drag me across town to this dump with the premise that you want to know all about my life, and you leave me alone for twenty minutes while you do coke in the bathroom?"

"It's not like it was crack or tina."

I looked at him, exasperated.

He put his arm around me. "You feel left out. Come on, I'll take you back there."

"Look, this isn't . . . we . . . us . . . you . . . " Runway looked at me, not understanding. "You and I, this isn't going to work."

He laughed hysterically; I noticed his hands trembling. "Lighten up, Curt. Let's blow this joint, go to my place, and do the damn thang."

"I'm light enough, you did blow this joint, my name is Curtis, I am not going back to your place, and I'm not doing the damn *thang* with you."

Not happy with what I said, he backed me up against the wall. But I held my ground and in my calmest voice, I said, "I liked Calvin. I want Calvin. I don't want Runway."

I thought his fist was going to go through the wall—through my face first, but through the wall.

"So now you are playing judge and jury. You spend the whole evening letting me expose myself to you. Telling you my deepest, darkest secrets, and now you find me guilty?"

I looked up at him, afraid to say a word.

"Well, if it's Calvin you want, it's Calvin you'll get," he boomed in a deep baritone voice. "We're leaving."

And with the strength of ten angry men, Calvin, wearing a white polyester pantsuit zipped down to his navel, a jacket-style mink coat, and carrying a clutch, grabbed my arm and dragged me toward the front door. I honestly feared he was going to rape and kill me. I was going to end up a statistic, a mere blurb among the crime reports in the New York Post: "Gay writer discovered slain, dismembered, and stuffed into trunk in Meadowlands."

That's when the bouncer came to my rescue—the bouncer, who was probably an inch taller than Runway, and two men wider.

My human straitjacket looked at him and slurred, "Hey, Tiny." All of a sudden, Runway's tongue started doing weird gymnastics, as though he was trying to blow bubble gum or something. "Meet my lover, Curt."

"I'm not your lover, and I'm not going home with you."

Tiny wedged his body between us. "Let go of the guy, Runway."

There was a split second when I actually thought Runway was going to slug it out with Tiny and then he released me.

I was scared and ready to duck.

"I'll let you go, Curt. But you're the loser." He started out the door and then turned back to me. "Just for the record, you're the guilty one."

He twirled around, preparing for his dramatic exit, but unfortunately for him, he caught his jacket-style mink coat on the door handle. Oblivious to the tear, Runway disappeared into the night.

Feeling a little bit wobbly, I sat back down at the bar and ordered a manhattan straight up with Marker's Mark.

I must learn from my mistakes. But how many more mistakes can I learn from? How was I supposed to know that Calvin was really Runway? I confess that I projected upon a total stranger, before even meeting him, my ideal of the perfect man. But if I am guilty of anything, it's of having an open heart and an inexhaustible hope and dream that somewhere out there is my soul mate.

With that optimistic outlook, I held up my drink and toasted myself: "Allz menz iz dawgz."

SEVEN

MAN-EATER

It had been two weeks since my last appointment with
Dr. Tunick, and I couldn't wait to see her. I literally ran from
my apartment to hers.

But typical for New York, the appropriate springlike weather
had changed dramatically. Although it was sunny and quite
mild, as I walked down West End Avenue, it started to snow, not
heavy or wet but light and fluffy. It all seemed quite enchanting,
as if we were being shaken up in a snow globe. At first I thought
they were dandelion seeds floating in the air, but as soon as one
melted on my nose, I knew they were a flakes.

A bit of advice: Never walk down a city block with your
nose in the air. That's when I tripped into her.

"Any change, sir? Any change today?" asked the bag lady.

I apologized and then threw money into her cup, whispering, "No, ma'am. No change today. Same old same old."

Once I was buzzed into Dr. Tunick's brownstone, I skipped
two steps at a time, past the second-floor parlor door that
creaked open and slammed shut, and bounded up to the third
floor.

Before I could even knock on Magda's door, I could hear
Emily-Mae's demonic growl. She could pee on me all she
wanted. I had had three dates.

≥ ≤

≳ ≲

Dr. Tunick was furious with me. Her oversized man foot was spinning around her thick ankle so fast I thought she was going to take flight.

"I told you to go out and date, not become a man-eater."

"But—"

She jumped to her feet, causing Emily-Mae to fall off her lap and onto the floor. My first reaction was to pick up the dog, but her needle-toothed snarl changed my mind.

Dr. Tunick paced the parlor. "I said to check out personals on the Internet, not sex chat rooms." She really was upset with me. "Your behavior was so cavalier; I'm surprised you weren't knifed to death."

"But . . ."

Emily-Mae had wandered over to the organ and was gnawing on the foot pedal when Dr. Tunick picked her up.

"As for Desifinado, it's obvious that you don't know your Spanish. The translation of his name is 'slightly out of tune.'"

She sat back down in her chair and placed the dog at her feet.

"But—"

"And when it comes to dating African-Americans? Let me be more articulate and less general." She leaned in toward me and whispered, "All black men have intimacy issues."

My jaw dropped. "You can't say things like that."

"Yes, I can. And I can say this, too. All white men are repressed." She took a very deep breath, paused, and seemed to have purged herself of the anger. "So, how do you feel?"

"Well, I felt great."

"You mean that what I just said deflated all your enthusiasm that quickly?"

"Something deflated?"

And then I heard it again. Dr. Tunick made a strange guttural sound from the back of her throat. It rang of such sarcasm that I couldn't let it go.

"That is so judgmental."

She shook her head and rolled her eyes as though she had her hands full.

At that moment, Emily-Mae approached my shoe, and I quickly guided her in the opposite direction.

Dr. Tunick thought for a moment and then asked me, "Would you characterize yourself as someone who has mood swings?"

Irritated, I had to get up out of my chair. "Doesn't everyone?"

"Extreme mood swings?"

I walked over to the mantel, the top of which was covered in picture frames. "Sometimes I can go from being ecstatic to down if—" I shot her a glance— "someone bursts my bubble."

"Blamer, too," she said out of the corner of her mouth.

I caught her glancing at her watch again.

"Stop doing this." I exaggerated looking at my watch.

"How does it make you feel?"

"Like you'd rather be with any other patient than me."

She took down a note and implied that I was not only paranoid but possibly bipolar as well.

I explained to her that it was true that every family member of mine was now on antidepressants, but that didn't necessarily mean that my brain chemistry was off. At least I hoped not, anyway.

But, honestly, at that moment I was more interested in the pictures on the mantel. Each and every one of them was a photo of an animal. There were cats and dogs and even a few birds. One had two hamsters in it, and another had a gigantic yellow boa constrictor. Each picture had indecipherable faded handwriting on it. I wondered if these had all been her pets.

"Curtis, tell me about your relationship with your siblings."

Sensing that this was going nowhere, I wondered how many more of these sessions I would have to endure.

"Stewie and Kelly? We don't talk much. I e-mail Stewie every so often. I have dinner with Kelly once, maybe twice, a year."

I wandered toward the front of the room.

"Does Kelly live far away?"

"Yes, the Upper East Side."

I explained to her that there was nothing wrong. Kelly and I never had a big falling-out or anything. We just didn't have much to say to each other.

"Strange," she muttered.

Annoyed at this condescending response, I spun around to confront her and slammed my foot into a heavy metal table. It took a moment before the pain registered. "There you go again, being judgmental," I whimpered.

"Aren't *you* in a pissy mood."

"Well, I wasn't until I got here."

She gestured for me to sit back down. "On the contrary, Curtis. I'm just supposed to make you feel."

She's doing a pretty good job of it, I thought as I limped back to my chair. I was so not into this that it took every ounce of energy in me just to focus in on her questions.

"Where is your brother, and what does he do?"

"Texas; he delivers organs. People's organs. Dead people's organs. Fast. Hopefully."

And then I noticed that the dress she was wearing today was quite form-fitting.

"Do you all get together for holidays, anniversaries, special occasions?"

I informed her that neither my sister nor my brother were on speaking terms with my mother.

Dr. Tunick reached across her chest to scratch her arm, and I noticed that she actually had very nice breasts.

"And your father?"

"No one speaks to him. He's dead. Oh, except for his sister, Aunt Tilly. She talks to him through her Ouija board."

In fact, her breasts seemed very high and round.

"How about when he was alive?"

"No, no one spoke to him, and he didn't speak to us."

"What did your father do?"

I smiled. "He was a brilliant scientist. I think he invented aluminum."

She eyed me very suspiciously and took more notes. Looking at her, I wondered if maybe she was wearing a special bra. Or maybe she had had a boob job? Her breasts were awfully perky.

"But you do speak to your mother?"

"Yes. In fact, she knows I'm in therapy, and I told her you had me on a mission to find a man."

Staring at her chest, I wondered if she still had sex.

"She's comfortable with you being gay?" She looked up from her notes and caught me checking her out. Her tone changed dramatically. "You are gay, aren't you?"

This was a really weird and awkward moment. Nervously, I laughed it off and confirmed that I was definitely gay and shared with her an event that clearly showed how comfortable my mother was with my sexual orientation.

≳ ≲

On one occasion, I was home from college on a break, and my mother dragged me, once more, to none other than the Purity Save More.

My father was at work, and my siblings were off somewhere. It wasn't a holiday or anyone's birthday. Yet, in my mother's mind, this trip to the supermarket was of the utmost importance. And it was very clear that the trip could not be made without me.

But once we got there, she went straight for a loaf of bread and a carton of milk, and that was it. Then she shoved me into the "twenty or more items" checkout lane, which happened to have a very long line of people in it.

So I naturally pointed to the express lane and suggested that we switch over.

"No, darling," she said firmly. "This is our register."

Knowing it was going to take forever, I tried to move over, but she blocked me, reiterating, "We are staying in this line."

I gave in. If there's one thing I've learned, there's usually a method to my mother's madness. Or should I say a madness to her madness? Anyway, I soon found out what it was.

Both she and I exchanged pleasantries with Candy, our cashier, but as she checked us out, I realized the bagboy was checking me out. He placed the milk and the bread into the sack carefully and methodically, and then he smiled dreamily at me like a puppy dog.

My mother jabbed me in the side with her elbow. "Say hello to Scooter."

"Hello, Scooter," I said tentatively to the pimple-faced, skinny boy with Coke-bottle eyeglasses who couldn't have been more than sixteen. My mother grabbed his arm and winked as I raced out of the store.

"Curtis, come back here."

She caught up with me at the car and said that my actions were totally unacceptable.

Clueless, I shrugged my shoulders, got into the car, and locked my door.

She ran around to the driver's side and jumped in. "You could have been a little bit nicer."

"To whom?"

She turned the key in the ignition so hard I thought it was going to break off. "Honestly, Curtis, you are such a snob."

"What are you talking about?"

She backed out of our parking space without looking and just missed hitting a woman and her baby. "Here I've been talking you up for over a month to Scooter, and I finally introduce you to him and you brush him off like he's a bagboy."

"Mother, he *is* a bagboy."

She tore through the parking lot. "I'm only trying to help you find someone."

"This is pathetic."

"What's wrong with Scooter?" she asked as she steered toward the Purity Save More entrance.

"He's jailbait?"

"He's very courteous."

She came to a screeching halt in front of the store.

"I'm not looking for courteous."

I looked to my right, and there was Scooter, holding the one small bag of bread and milk. My mother unlocked my door. I opened it, quickly grabbed the bag, thanked him, and then shut the door.

Scooter walked away looking dejected.

"I hope you're proud of yourself, *Curtis*," she said, seething. "I can never go back there again."

I just rolled my eyes as she sped off.

≷ ≷

I looked at Dr. Tunick, who was looking at me in disbelief.

"So, as you can see, my mother is very comfortable with me being gay."

Dr. Tunick was reflective for a few moments. When she asked me how my mother felt about me being HIV-positive, her tone had shifted. She sounded very maternal.

"My mother's much better about it now."

"Was she devastated when you told her?"

I laughed. "Yes, devastated when I told her that I told Quinn first. She went on and on about how I could keep it from her and then tell a non-family member first.

"How could you, Curtis?"

I told Dr. Tunick that I was tested during a time that, if you came up positive, it was a death sentence. My doctor and I figured I had maybe five years left, tops. I had so many fears to deal with, so many things to put in order before it was "my time."

"This may sound selfish, but I asked myself, If I tell my mother now, would it help me? And my answer was no."

"Actually, Curtis, that wasn't being selfish, it was being healthy." She smiled at me so warmly, so nonjudgmentally.

"Thank you." I just realized this was the first time Dr. Tunick made any reference to me either doing the right thing or being healthy. For a moment, I looked at her and thought I was seeing my own grandmother. And suddenly the floodgates opened up.

She handed me the box of tissues.

I blew my nose and composed myself. "I'm sorry. I just thought of my granny, my mother's mom. I miss her very much. I never talked to her about my sexual orientation, but there was a quiet understanding. And I chose never to reveal my health status to her. The last thing she said to me just before having her last and final stroke was, 'I pray that you collide into your soul mate. But in the meantime, dear, please play safe.' She was cool, to say the least." I paused. "And I think you are, too."

Dr. Tunick was obviously very moved by this. She took a moment and then recovered by declaring, "If this is an act of transference, it's got to stop right now."

We both laughed and I looked at my watch.

"I guess my time is up."

"Is it already?" She smiled as Emily-Mae walked me to the door. "Same time, two weeks from today?"

I smiled back at her. "And with at least two more dates."

By the time I had left her building, it had stopped snowing. I slowly walked uptown on Broadway, thinking that my journey so far with Dr. Tunick had been different, to say the least. But I wondered, did I really need a shrink to help me find a man? Were my choices that far off? Was I attracted to the wrong types or looking in the wrong places? Wasn't I mature enough to handle this all on my own?

My mind was made up. As soon as I got home, I was going to call Magda and cancel my next appointment. I was going to say it'd been wonderful meeting and working with her but that I'm really okay on my own.

Feeling self-confident and relieved, I stopped in at my favorite Korean market to pick up a few items.

But when I entered I had to do a double take. Was this a gay bar? Better yet, a gay cruise ship? Years ago, the Upper West Side was definitely our neighborhood, housing plenty of actors, dancers, and singers, but nowadays I referred to it as suburbia. We had been replaced with triple strollers.

Hence, it was strange to see so many gay men at one time in a store up here. Beautiful gay men, I might add. Talk about a fruit stand. I didn't know where to begin. Everything looked so fresh.

I was just about to reach for a peach to see how firm it was when suddenly a red-haired stud extended his arm right in front of my face and picked the fruit I was eyeing. His huge and bulging biceps flexed so close to my face they almost knocked me over.

Nervous that he might choose again quickly, I grabbed any old peach and threw it into my basket.

I moved over to the oranges and picked one up to see if it had substantial weight. I lightly tossed it up into the air and then noticed a pretty blond Twinkie smiling at me. I smiled back self-consciously and dropped the orange. I quickly picked it up and threw that into my basket as well.

Embarrassed, I moved over to the melons. I chose a big, heavy one and knocked on it. I wasn't sure what I was supposed to be listening for, but I pretended to know.

I also smelled my fruit to make sure it was sweet. Sensing that I had an audience, I sniffed the rock-hard honeydew and looked up at the sexy-daddy type that was watching me. Knowingly, I smiled and put the melon in my basket. I smelled nothing.

I looked all around the store and realized that I was an equal-opportunity fruit picker. It didn't matter if it was green, yellow, orange, red, purple, or even pink. Honestly, I love all fruit.

There was a long line of men waiting to check out, and each one seemed more tempting than the next. Without watching where I was walking, I tripped.

Luckily, an overdeveloped forearm appeared from out of the line of men, offering me support and preventing me from falling on my face. But the person it was attached to was oblivious to me and mesmerized by a boyfriend.

I retreated to the back of the line. Eventually, I paid for my fruit, and once back outside on the sidewalk, I saw the pretty blond again. He was looking right at me and smiling so hard. I got excited and full of anticipation as he walked toward me. And then my heart sank. He wasn't smiling at me at all. He passed me and embraced a big furry bear type behind me.

I walked home. Once in my apartment, I threw the grocery bag onto the kitchen counter and the peach rolled out. I washed it off.

All too often I bring what I think is an absolutely perfect specimen of fruit home, only to find out—I took a big bite out of the peach and made an awful face—that it's bruised and mushy on the inside. I threw the fruit into the trash and kept my next appointment with Dr. Tunick.

EIGHT

STARFUCKER

"I can't believe I'm barhopping with my mother."

"Dear, you know I have the best gaydar in town."

I was tempted to bring up Scooter as we strolled arm in arm up Ninth Avenue, but I didn't.

She looked at the people we were passing. "Now, let's find you a real man."

The two of us had just seen a Broadway show and I had treated her to dinner at Joe Allen's. My mother not only spotted Natasha Richardson, Nathan Lane, and Bebe Neuwirth in the restaurant, she went up to each and every one of them, introduced herself, and ordered me to take pictures of her with all of them. *Couldn't an autograph suffice?*

Actually, I did the same thing, but to just one actress: Cherry Jones. I am my mother's son, for goodness' sake. This ordeal, though, was more than a full night out for me, but not for my mother.

"Curtis, what is this part of town called?"

"Hell's Kitchen."

"I love it. It's so gay and festive." She picked up her speed and spread her arms wide, leaving me in the dust. "It has a theatrical feel. Almost bohemian, like the Village used to be."

She was right on the mark. The gay ghetto moved from the Village to Chelsea in the mid- 1980s. Now it was very clear that the west 40s and 50s were becoming the next stomping ground.

I liked to call it Hellsea.

"Mother, I can only hit one bar. I have to write tomorrow."

"You're such a poop," she said as we entered Chaste, a cocktail lounge located on 55th Street.

I quickly took off my glasses and shoved them into my pocket. I admired the way she could walk into a room and feel absolutely unself-conscious and totally *her*.

"Howdy, boys!" she hollered.

And believe it or not, they all hollered howdy back. What can I say? She's a party girl.

Walking into this bar always felt like entering someone's digestive tract. The front had a long, narrow neck, and then all of a sudden you plopped into this big, round belly of a room.

We found two seats at the bar and quickly ordered our drinks.

"Is there anybody here, Mother?"

"Put on your damned glasses. I feel like your Seeing Eyedog."

"Men don't make passes at men who wear glasses."

"Darling," she said, exasperated, "go rent *How to Marry a Millionaire*."

She asked me why I didn't wear contact lenses, and I explained that my eyes absorb the moisture out of them. Last time I put a pair in, the ophthalmologist had to peel them off with tweezers.

My mother screamed, not because of how painful that sounded but because of the gorgeous hunk at the end of the bar.

She pointed to him. "There's one for you, Curtis."

I squinted as hard as I could, but I couldn't see where he was, what he looked like, or what he was wearing.

She waved to this man and he smiled back.

"But what kind of guy does he look like?"

"Brown hair, blue eyes, and the kind of man you'd bring home to your mother." She pushed me off of my stool. "Hurry, dear."

"But he's smiling at *you*, not me."

"Don't worry, you look just like me." She fiddled with my hair. "Go get him, slugger."

She downed her drink and put on her coat. No way was she going to leave me like this, so I put my coat back on, too.

"Curtis, my job is done," she said as she pulled it off. "Besides, I have to catch the twelve-twenty train back home."

She kissed me on the cheek and pushed me in his direction. "Now, don't be shy. Just say hello and smile."

"But—"

"Good night, Dear. Call me tomorrow and don't do anything I wouldn't do." She laughed as she left me.

Don't do anything she wouldn't? That means anything's game.

She tried to leave the bar right away, but I noticed men left and right stopping her to talk and giggle.

I took a big gulp of my drink and worked my way to the end of the bar. In the process, one man cursed at me for stepping on his toes, another threatened to send me his dry-cleaning bill after I spilled my drink on him, and a third wanted to punch my lights out when I stared at his boyfriend too long. I thought it was the man at the end of the bar.

Finally, I squeezed in next to my mother's gorgeous hunk. He did have brown hair and blue eyes, and was smiling at me, but up close he looked very plain. His face reminded me of an artist's blank canvas.

"It's pretty crowded in here tonight!" I shouted.

"Sure is!" he hollered back.

We both looked painfully around the room.

"So, my name is Curtis."

"Bartlett."

"I beg your pardon?

"My name is Bartlett, as in pear."

How unusual. In fact, a bit too unusual, so I slithered away from the bar to put my coat back on when I noticed that his body was actually shaped just like a pear.

I was just about to say good-bye to him when I saw a piece of paper on the bar. It was a note addressed to Bartlett and signed Liza Minnelli.

I know this sounds like a cliché, me being a gay man and all, but I love Liza almost as much as I love Judy. In fact, I'll never forget when I saw her at the Winter Garden Theater way back in the 70s. Actually, it was one of the few times Kelly and I went to the theater together.

It was after the movie *Cabaret* and the TV special *Liza with a Z*. And she was phenomenal. She took no less then eleven curtain calls. We wouldn't let her leave. Even the elegant, sophisticated woman who had been sitting in front of me wearing a mink coat stood up on her seat, screaming, "Liza!"

So, it's understandable that I just had to ask Bartlett what this note was all about.

"Oh, that?" he said in a blasé tone. "Liza was just thanking me again for all my work."

"Really? What kind of work do you do for her?"

"I'm the self-appointed, unofficial president of Liza's online fan club."

Well, as you can imagine, I was captivated. For the next thirty minutes he shared the hottest and juiciest gossip. He had inside info about her gay husbands and lovers, the numerous miscarriages, and the drug addictions dating way back to her stint in *The Fantastiks*. He also gave me more recent reports on her failing health and loss of vocal cords. But then he teased me with dirt about her beating up exes and bodyguards and then abruptly stated that he had to go to bed.

"I always leave early on Friday mornings to go to my weekend house in the Hamptons."

My ears perked way up. Sometimes my own shallowness

frightens me.

"You have a weekend house in the Hamptons?"

Suddenly, Bartlett kissed me, and it wasn't a bad one at that.

"Curtis," he asked, "would you like to come out to the beach? No strings attached, unless you'd like it that way."

He suggested that we could walk along the water and then sit in front of a roaring fire in the fireplace.

I thought, what an invitation. Plus, he offered to show me all of his Liza memorabilia.

"It sounds very tempting, Bartlett."

"I know," he said seductively. "And so am I."

He kissed me again and slipped me his card.

≷ ≷

That Friday I rode the West 86th Street crosstown bus east to catch the Jitney to the Hamptons. I got off at Lexington Avenue and wondered to myself as I looked around what had happened to the Upper East Side.

Granted, there were still prestigious addresses in that area, but besides my sister, Kelly, I didn't know a living soul who lived over there. Believe it or not, my neighborhood had become more desirable. People now look in the east 80s and north for apartment bargains.

If I had taken the Jitney bus, before I would have known to get there a little bit earlier then I did. It was packed solid. And once onboard, everyone was yakking on cell phones, including me to my mother.

"Speak up, Curtis, I can just barely hear you."

From the funky sound of music in the background and a glance at my watch, I realized that she was in the middle of her Jazzercise class at her local Westchester women's gym.

The odd thing about cell phones is how much they pick up

and magnify background noise. I guess it's nature's way of preparing us for what it will be like to wear hearing aids after the cell phones make us deaf.

I covered the mouthpiece with my hand. "I have grave reservations about going to a stranger's house."

She was really huffing and puffing. "There's a male substitute instructor today, a Jamaican hottie named Taboo."

I looked around to see whether anyone was listening to me on the bus. "I'm breaking one of my cardinal rules. First date, just drinks in my city."

"Curtis, you already had drinks in your city," she reminded me. "Where's your sense of adventure?" I could hear the women in her class shouting catcalls at Taboo. "And if it doesn't work out with Bartlett, think of all the attractive, wealthy friends he could introduce you to out in the Hamptons."

I wondered if my mother was really a gay man trapped in a straight woman's body.

"Dear, have fun." The class was beginning to roar. "But if I don't hear from you by tomorrow night, I'm calling Liza."

"Mother . . . "

I heard her scream, "Tabooty, I love you!" and then she hung up. I prayed she wasn't going to give herself a coronary.

≥ ≤

For some reason, getting off of the Jitney threw me back to getting off the school bus as a child. My mother would be waiting for me, screaming my name and embarrassing me in front of all the kids. But this time it was Bartlett screaming my name and embarrassing me in front of all the adults going to the "guest Hamptons."

"Curtis!" he hollered. "Curtis, I'm over here!"

He was standing next to the most spectacular red convertible sport Mercedes I had ever seen in my life. I quickly dragged my bag over to him and stood next to the car, admiring it.

"Beauty, isn't it?" he asked.

I'm not even into cars, but this one was stunning. I had to run my hand across her. "How much did it cost, Bartlett?"

"No idea," he said as he opened the door of the car next to it. His car was a rusted, falling-apart Chevy Impala circa 1970. Was this the beginning of the end?

I don't remember much of what he chatted about during the ride back to his house. Most of my energy was spent slumping down in the passenger seat far enough so that no one who could possibly know me could possibly see me.

As I peeked out of the window, I saw us pass one mansion after another until we finally turned into a dark and densely wooded driveway. We had made our way to Bartlett's very own mansion.

"Here we are, Curtis," he declared with great pride. "Home sweet home."

It was a trailer. He lived in a trailer in the Hamptons? Is that legal?

The only thing worse than the outside of his abode, which did have a cracked bathtub sitting on the front lawn, was the inside.

Less than spotless, this tiny trailer was jam-packed with Liza crap. On one wall was a cheap Andy Warhol print reproduction of Liza's portrait. On tables and bookshelves were Liza lunch boxes, Liza key chains, and Liza paper-doll books. Three life-size look a like Liza mannequins wore Liza costumes from *Flora the Red Menace*, *A Sterile Cuckoo*, and *The Act!* And lovingly laid out on his kitchen counter was his collection of Liza dolls.

And I can't forget Toto. Bartlett had a stuffed terrier, just like the one in *The Wizard of Oz*.

"Liza has a Toto, too," he giggled. "But a live one."

A quick scan of that hellhole revealed no fireplace, and when confronted about it, he laughed it off and said there was one in town at a restaurant.

And when I asked about the walks on the beach, he nonchalantly suggested we could drive to the water if I really needed to see it. I knew I was going to need help and prayed that he had some Maker's Mark.

"Only Blue Nun," he said proudly.

"Blue Nun?"

"Sweet white wine? Judy drank it all the time. Now Liza does."

Mother, I could kill you right now. As Bartlett pulled out his Liza photo album, I pulled out the Jitney bus schedule back to New York City.

"You'll love how I've arranged this book. On one page is Liza, on the opposite page is me."

He patted the orange plastic kitchen banquette cushion next to himself, encouraging me to join him. I pushed three Lizas out of the way.

Bartlett randomly opened the scrapbook. He pointed to a picture on the left page of Liza smoking at Studio 54.

"And what is this?" I asked pointing to a picture on the other page.

"Me at the Roxy, with a cigarette."

"You smoke?" I asked with a tone letting him know that he was now history. I was off the hook. Check, please.

"No. Not anymore. Liza stopped."

I just looked at Bartlett as he continued. Flipping through, he stopped at a picture of himself when he was at least twenty pounds heavier. On the opposite page was a bloated Liza. It turns out she was stressed from feuding with Lorna and she'd overdosed on mashed potatoes and gravy.

"Judy's favorite, too," Bartlett added.

This was too fucking weird.

He came across a bunch of wallet-sized pictures taken of

him just a few weeks ago. Eager to have me remember him, he slipped one into my pocket. There was no way in hell I was going to forget him.

As he flipped through the album, a pamphlet for Lifespring fell out.

"Isn't this like EST?" I asked.

"Yes, it's an offshoot," Bartlett said, "Liza took Lifespring so . . ."

"You took it, too."

"Yes, and I feel so much more complete and empowered. Now I'm an individual not influenced by other people," Bartlett boasted with pride.

This man needs a reality check.

But when I thought it couldn't get any worse, Bartlett informed me that he had a big surprise. He ran to his tape player and put on an obscure, rough bootleg recording of Liza.

"It's live, and I have the only copy," he whispered, as though the cops where on his trail.

"Where was it done?"

"Rainbow Mountain in the Poconos."

This gay resort is actually quite wonderful. You can stay in old-fashioned cabins, and the restaurant is exceptional. There's a pool and a huge barn. Downstairs, one can play pool or sing karaoke, and upstairs is a dance floor. Some fun and talented entertainers make it out there, but it's a sad day for Liza if she's working this joint in the Pennsylvania mountains.

Bartlett popped some pills into his mouth. "Liza had to recently cancel her national nightclub tour because her hip replacement was bothering her." He limped toward his bedroom and groaned, "I'll be out in a second."

I listened to Liza try to sing "New York, New York," "Maybe This Time," and something I'd never heard her do before, "Over the Rainbow." But considering how lackluster the audience was applauding on the pirate tape, I think the Rainbow Mountain was over Liza.

It was while I was looking at a glass box full of her real hair and fingernail clippings that Bartlett finally emerged from his bedroom.

"Sorry," he cooed, "Liza is always late for her engagements."

Now I knew why Bartlett had a blank canvas for a face. Give him some Max Factor and a paintbrush, and Andy Warhol watch out. He came out of his bedroom in full Liza drag.

"Come to me, Curtis," he half-sang with a warbling vibrato. "Come make love to Liza."

Shocked and repulsed, I couldn't get out of there fast enough. I literally ran all the way back to the Jitney bus stop.

≳ ≲

The next day I ordered my mother to come into the city and meet me for brunch. I wanted to tell her this story, face-to-face.

She suggested several extremely popular restaurants in my neighborhood, but there's one thing I will not do in New York City, and that's wait in line outside for a table. Instead, I told her to meet me at wonderful Peruvian place just north of my apartment on Amsterdam Avenue.

As was typical, my mother was late, so by the time she got there, I had already ordered a seviche that was to die for. And while gazing out the window, I thought to myself how amazing it was that just ten years ago, this stretch of Amsterdam from 87th Street on up to 96th Street was a virtual wasteland except for struggling bodegas and down-and-out drug dealers. Now it had been transformed into "restaurant row," boasting some really exceptional establishments.

Once she had arrived and ordered, I filled her in on all the details.

"Liza in drag?" she pondered as she devoured her avocado-and-shrimp appetizer. "Isn't that redundant?"

"Mother, I can't believe you talked me into going."

She looked up at the ceiling and made a funny face.

"Those are Peruvian Nazca figures painted up there, and don't you dare try to change the subject."

She defended herself. "I didn't talk you into anything. Besides, I still think he was cute."

I took the wallet-sized picture of Bartlett out of my pocket and threw it onto the table.

"If you think he's so cute, then you fuck Liza Minnelli."

She picked up the picture and stared at it.

"Who's this?" she asked.

I was tired of playing games. "Who the hell do you think it is?"

"This is the guy you went to visit in the Hamptons?"

"Yes, he's the one you pointed out to me in the bar."

"Curtis," she said, using every ounce of control in her body not to laugh, "I was pointing to the guy next to him."

NINE

GOT ANY GUM ON YA, DICK?

I had arrived for my next session with Dr. Tunick about fifteen minutes early on purpose. Although it was a warm, sunny day out, my mind felt dark and cloudy.

My literary agent had just asked me to leave his office in a not-so-very-friendly fashion. Unhappy with the way he had recently negotiated a contract for a regional production of one of my plays and not feeling that I was high on their list of priority clients, I exercised my right to end my contract with the office. The negative response and harsh words were quite a surprise to me.

With a simple half-caf grande hazelnut caramel mocha latte topped with whipped cream in hand, I sat down on the park bench across from Magda's house to collect my thoughts before the appointment. One sip and I heard her heavy European accent bellow out to me.

She waved from her front parlor window, said she had an emergency, and asked if I could come on up. A bit panicked, I jumped to my feet and was in her apartment in a flash.

The problem was Emily-Mae. It turns out that she had an ongoing liver disorder. Periodically, she needed an intravenous hydration, and Dr. Tunick needed an extra pair of hands to help with the process.

Once we were set up to do it, we had to find the dog. Twenty minutes later, Dr. Tunick discovered her in the linen closet warming up next to a hot-water pipe. With time running out, she decided to do our session while hydrating Emily-Mae.

"I hate Liza Minnelli," declared Dr. Tunick quite emphatically.

"*Hate* is an awfully strong word," I said.

Magda had an IV bag full of lactated Ringer's solution hooked to a stand next to her chair. She said that Emily-Mae was calmer sitting on her lap than up on a table. I sat at the foot of her chair and petted the dog as she prepared the needle.

"And I really hated her mother."

"Judy Garland?"

I looked at the size of the needle and guessed it to be a 13-gauge. Dr. Tunick was surprised that I knew that. I informed her that my next-door neighbor had a cat that she had to hydrate every day for almost a year, and I frequently assisted her.

"Don't know what people saw in Judy," she continued.

"I think they saw talent and beauty; her life was an open book."

"Curtis, she was homely, drug-addicted, and just to watch her made me nervous."

"Okay, you made your point."

Speaking of points, Magda grabbed the scruff of Emily-Mae's neck and gently but firmly tried to push the big, thick needle through her skin. Her first attempt was a failure, so we just rested for a moment.

She then threw me for a loop by asking me if I was jealous of my mother. I had no idea where she had come up with that one.

"When you described how she walked into that bar and how all the men responded to her, you certainly had a strong reaction to that."

"Yes, I was embarrassed."

"And jealous?"

I confessed that I might have been somewhat envious of her

ability not to care what anybody thinks about her, but jealous I certainly was not.

Dr. Tunick pulled Emily-Mae by the scruff again, but the needle wouldn't puncture the skin. It was as if it were hitting a brick wall.

Magda pulled it out, causing Emily-Mae to yelp, and that's when I saw her hand trembling. It wasn't because she couldn't do it or because she didn't have the digital dexterity. Clearly, she was emotionally upset.

I casually offered to do it. She looked at me incredulously, but I reassured her that I was pretty good at it.

Emily-Mae's skin had probably become callused, and we needed to enter from a new area. And sometimes a new needle could be dull, so I exchanged it for another one.

As she held the dog, I pulled up the skin and inserted the needle. I felt the gentle puncture, relaxed the skin, and the solution began dripping right away. To tell you the truth, I've always had a morbid fascination with needles. I should have been a phlebotomist, or at the very least a heroin addict.

If Dr. Tunick was impressed, she certainly didn't show it. She just plowed on. "Are you terribly self-conscious, Curtis?"

"Well, I . . ."

She wanted to know if I constantly watched and censored myself.

That was my mother's problem. She had no censoring mechanism, and, living in a civilized society, you can't just go around blurting out anything and everything you think and feel.

"You can't?" Dr. Tunick asked me seriously.

"I give up."

Angry, I sat there in silence, petting Emily-Mae. She was responding so quickly to the hydration and had that happy, dreamy, "I'm about to take a nap" look in her eyes. That relaxed me.

Dr. Tunick finally asked me what was wrong.

"I'm not going to fight with you," I said very calmly.

"Is that what you think we are doing?"

"We aren't agreeing."

She explained to me that just because I didn't agree with her, it didn't mean we were fighting.

"You're right, I'm wrong." I pouted. "I'm jealous of my mother. She's together, I'm not. Are you happy now?"

"There's no need to be childishly black and white."

I raised my voice. "So now I'm childish and black and white? Amazing, and to think I'm paying for this."

The hair on Emily-Mae's back stood up.

"If you want me to agree with you on everything, I can, Curtis. But you won't make any progress."

I got up from the floor and started pacing the room. She had me cornered. My first reaction was to bolt, but I didn't. I took a deep breath.

"Curtis? Why do you get so upset when someone thinks or acts differently from you?"

I thought hard, but the words just wouldn't come together. "Because . . . because . . . because I want people to like me?"

"And you think they won't if you have a different opinion?"

I was so confused I started rubbing my head, so she suggested we shift. After a moment, she asked me whether I had had any other dates.

On a gut level, I hesitated to say yes but then just went for it. Embarrassed, I confessed that I had met a man in Riverside Park. But I was quick to tell her that it wasn't in any of the trashy areas. It was at the garden at the end of the promenade located near 91st Street.

She laughed, saying it was okay, wherever I met him.

⋛ ⋚

It was cold enough to wear gloves, but it felt invigorating. And the garden was already in full bloom with its spring flowers and greenery. The sun was still rising a bit low in the horizon so I took a seat at the south end of the park. With no one else around, it was the perfect setting to enjoy my copy of D. H. Lawrence's short stories.

"I love his writing," he said, startling me.

I looked up, but all I saw was the silhouette of a man standing before me. I put my hand up to my brow like a visor and tried to focus.

He stepped aside, and I'm sure I let out a gasp. He was an exquisitely beautiful Japanese boy.

Speechless, he continued to tell me that he really liked Lawrence's story about a married woman who goes to Italy with just her young child and discovers the joy of nude sunbathing.

I offered him a seat next to me and informed him that I hadn't gotten to that one yet.

We sat there for a bit, and then he broke the tension-filled silence with, "I love social nudism."

"How old are you?" I asked.

"Twenty-one, and you?"

"Old enough to be your father." I cringed. "And what the hell is social nudism?"

An example he offered was nude camping and hiking.

I let out a disapproving grunt. "You can't hike in the nude."

"I know a guy who goes to Vermont, and he says he hikes in the nude." He flashed me a devilish smile. "He wants to take me there."

"What if you slip on a steep mountainside and get stabbed in the groin with a stick?" I exclaimed. "Or what if a family with children is coming down the trail and they see a stark-naked man?"

"Well, he says there are gay areas."

"He's a pervert."

We sat there not talking, which allowed my temper to cool. I glanced at him. He was so young and fresh and eager.

Point-blank, he stated, "I like older men." He moved a little closer. "I'd like to lose my virginity with an older man."

I broke into nervous laughter.

He suggested we go down to a really secluded place in the bushes, past the bike lane along the river.

This infuriated me. "What is your name?"

"Dickie."

"Hello, Dickie. I'm Curtis, and why the hell would you want to do it out in the open?"

He shrugged his shoulders.

I looked hard at this beautiful boy/man. "Are you really a virgin?"

"Yes."

"Are you attracted to me?"

"Yes. Are you attracted to me?"

"Yes."

He got up and looked at me. "Then let's go into the bushes and—"

"No," I stopped him. "If we're going to do it, we're going to do it indoors."

I suggested that since it was supposedly his first time, it should be nice and comfortable—an experience he could look back on with fond memories.

"Okay," Dickie said flatly.

I was more comfortable asking him to my apartment, but it was in the process of having new windows installed. So he offered his home, which was just up the steep hill on 94th Street and Riverside.

As we headed to his place, I admitted to myself that it was just going to be a onetime thing. No way in hell could I get involved with a child whom I was twice as old as.

"Do you happen to have a mint on you, Dickie?" I asked.

"No, but I do have some gum."

He gave me a stick and I thought to myself, *When and if I ever do die, my tombstone will read, Here Lies Curtis Jenkins, Who Died Of Mintitus.* I'm obsessed with my breath. Obsessed with it being bad. Hence, I always have a mint in the back of my mouth.

His building wasn't too far from mine. We rode up the elevator to the penthouse without saying a word. We walked in; it was magnificent, to say the least. The only thing more beautiful than the décor was the view. Every single window had a spectacular view of the Hudson River.

"Dickie, this is awesome."

"Thanks," he said as he held my hand and walked me down the hallway.

I asked him what he did for a living.

"My father is a record producer. I work with him, associate producing, while I go to NYU."

"Well, there's certainly a lot of money to be made in that industry."

"Tell me about it." He smiled as he pulled me into his bedroom.

In a flash, our clothes were off and we were lip-locked. He was ravenous and devouring me. I could barely keep up.

I don't think I had ever touched such a hairless, soft-skinned body in my life. Within moments he whispered that he wanted me inside of him. It was then that I remembered that I had forgotten to even mention my health status.

"I'm HIV-positive."

"I'm cool with that. Do you have a condom?"

I laughed. "No, I don't walk around with them on me."

However, I do know plenty of men and women who do.

He was cool with keeping things just oral. His body was so boyish and clean. It reminded me of freshly baked bread, and I was starving.

I pulled away from his mouth and started kissing him all over. His chest. His nipples. His stomach. His navel. And then I slipped him into my mouth. Both of us were consumed with passion when all of a sudden, the gum that I kept in the back of my mouth between my molar and my cheek, where I always stored my mint, dropped down and landed on Dickie's dick.

With one quick suction, I knew I could swoop up the gum and stick it back up in the corner of my mouth, but it didn't budge. I stopped all movement.

"Is everything okay, Curtis?"

"Yup," I mumbled.

Furiously, I worked with my tongue to get the fucking gum off his dick. Meanwhile, Dickie was writhing with pleasure and ecstasy.

"Curtis, what did you do? Go to sex school?"

"No, Dickie, I'm forty-five," I said with my mouth full.

He moaned as I feverishly worked to remove the gum.

Just then a door slammed shut. Both he and I lay there, frozen.

"Dickie?" asked a female voice.

"*Shit,*" he whispered. "My ma's home."

"Mother?" I choked. "You live with your mother?"

Needless to say, I panicked. Dickie threw me under his bed as he jumped under the covers.

She popped her head in through the doorway and I held my breath as I noticed my clothes on the floor next to the bed.

Dickie's mother frowned and asked why he was in bed when it was so nice out. He feigned being sick a little too well, because it prompted her to enter the bedroom.

Her feet were right at my face. I thought I was going to shit in my pants, but I wasn't wearing any.

She felt his forehead. "You do seem hot, dear."

God, if she only knew.

"Dickie, let me change, and then I'll take your temperature."

"No need to, Ma." He coughed as he held the covers tight to his body. "Really, I'm okay."

"Nonsense. Don't want you coming down with something."

She left the room, and I frantically threw on my clothes. First I put my pants on backward, then I put two legs in one pant leg. Then I couldn't get my shirt on because it was inside out.

Finally, Dickie scurried me into the kitchen and out the back door just as his mother was coming in.

"Son," she exclaimed, "you haven't a stitch of clothing on."

Dickie had forgotten, covering his crotch with his hands. She ordered him to march right back into bed before he made himself sicker.

Their voices faded away as I caught my breath in the back stairwell. I put my clothes on properly and then realized that I had everything but my shoes and socks.

So, on this cold and windy day, I slipped out the service entrance of Dickie's building and ran the four blocks east and one avenue north back to my house with my feet stuck into my gloves.

⋛ ⋜

"Curtis?" Dr. Tunick couldn't stop laughing. "That is so funny."

"No, it's not!" I cried out. "It's my life."

"I'm not only picturing you running past all these people with your gloves on your feet—" she was laughing so hard she started to snort— "but just imagine poor Dickie's face when he saw what was stuck to his penis."

She was right; it was funny. And I had to laugh. Which made her laugh harder, till tears were running down her cheeks.

"Oh, dear!" she said as she caught her breath. "You are something."

"I'll take that as a compliment."

Then she noticed that Emily-Mae's IV bag was empty, so she gently removed the needle from the back of her neck. It was always a bit disconcerting to see an animal after hydration. The liquids are injected just under the skin and pool down the front legs.

Dr. Tunick picked her up and set her on the floor. Emily-Mae wobbled away with huge saddlebags bouncing around her elbows. We both looked at her and then at each other and broke out into laughter again.

After we had regained our composure, she asked me, "Why, when the man who told Dickie of the place in Vermont where he gets naked out of doors, why did you call him a pervert?"

"Because he was one."

"Just because he likes to hike in the nude?"

It didn't take a rocket scientist to figure out that that's not what he was doing. It was obviously a place where gays hung out to have sex in the bushes. Just like Dickie had suggested to me.

Dr. Tunick confronted me. "What is so wrong with that?"

I explained to her that, first, we would have frozen our asses off. Second, it would have been degrading and demeaning and just plain . . . wrong.

"Curtis, where is all of this coming from?"

I shrugged my shoulders.

"Having sex out of doors can be a wonderful and liberating experience."

"Are you condoning what these men are doing in the bushes?"

"No, but your knee-jerk, irrational reaction to it is overreactive." I started to squirm in my seat. "You yourself have even admitted that no one is allowed to see you naked in the gym locker room, a place where it would be expected of you."

"And is it expected of me to have sex in the showers?"

"I didn't say that."

God, I hated this. I felt like a trapped animal.

"What is it that you are so upset about?"

I couldn't speak.

"Curtis, have you ever had sex in a public space?"

"I . . . I . . . I . . ." And then I just blurted it out. "Yes, the first time I had sex was in a public place. There, are you pleased?"

She encouraged me to go on. God, I really hated this. I stared at her, thinking of ways that I could get out of this, and then I realized the time. I pointed to my watch.

She shook her head, smiling, and said, "Just take your time."

≥ ≤

When I was seventeen, my family decided to rent a summerhouse for two weeks at Sandpiper Beach, a beautiful stretch of shore close to Montauk, Long Island.

Although I never really learned to swim, I was a water baby. I thoroughly enjoyed sitting, playing, or wading in it. Whenever I was near the water, it was hard to keep me out of it.

On the second day of our vacation, the ocean was warm and calm. I sat in the sand, close enough to the water so that the gentle waves would break and just barely touch my big boxer-style bathing suit.

In the distance I saw a group of young men playing football in the sand. One in particular stood out. Not only because he was Latino, tan, tall, and very attractive but also because he was the only man on the beach wearing a bikini. He entranced me.

At some point, the game ended and the men went off in different directions.

It being low tide, I waded through the thigh-high water, quite a distance out for me. No one was near and I was just enjoying the soothing undulation of the tide when all of a sudden the man in the bikini literally appeared out of the water in front of me. He had a full erection, and it was sticking straight up out of the waistband of his suit.

No words were spoken, although I do remember trembling. I followed him out of the water and onto the crowded beach. At this point my erection was laden down and camouflaged by my huge suit, but I wondered how he was hiding his.

His long, black locks cascaded down his chiseled back, and the way that his skimpy, powder-blue suit clung to his buns nearly caused me to suffer an aneurism. Hypnotized, I continued to follow him from several paces behind, into the dunes. I had never been up there before and was surprised to see so many trails.

He led me to a section where four trees protected an area so that a soft bed of sea grass could grow. It was beautiful. And so was he. He slid off his suit, and there he stood in all his glory. I was shaking even harder now. I clumsily pulled down my suit and was petrified when I realized that due to all the excitement, I had to go to the bathroom. And I don't mean pee.

He laid down on the grass and started stroking himself, silently indicating that he wanted me to go down on him. Obedient, I did so. He didn't touch me or kiss me. He didn't even make any sounds. And before I knew it, he pulled my head away from him and he shot all over my face. Blinded in one eye, I saw him quickly put his suit back on.

The only thing he said to me was, "Count to a hundred, then come out. I don't want my wife seeing you."

He climbed out of the dunes as I hunted for my suit, my eye stinging like crazy.

Disappointed, frightened, and confused, I had no control over my body and I had to evacuate. That's when I heard the clicking. From a distance, I saw a nerdy-looking man dressed in khakis and wearing a pith helmet, as if on a Safari, taking pictures of me.

I screamed at him to stop, but he wouldn't. I hastily finished my business, pulled up my suit, and he was gone. I had never been so humiliated in my entire life. For the rest of our stay at Sandpiper Beach, I never went near the water again.

≥ ≤

"So, Dr. Tunick, my first time was in a public place."

And up from the depths of my gut came this uncontrollable emotion. My legs were no longer able to support me; I crumpled to the rug and started to cry. I wailed like a baby. She got up out of her chair and held me.

"Congratulations, Curtis, you're on a journey. A journey of healing."

I don't know how long she rocked me while I cried, but I do remember Emily-Mae coming over and, sensing my pain, starting to lick my hand and whimper.

TEN

THE LADIES WHO LUNCH

Although I am absolutely, positively certain that cell phones give you cancer, I do use one myself, but as sparingly as possible. And it's sad to say that riding a New York City bus is now like sitting in the middle of a production of *Bells Are Ringing*. Phones are constantly going off with obnoxious ring tones like "Here Comes the Bride" or "Mary Had A Little Lamb" or—my least favorite to date—the "Woody Woodpecker" theme song.

But I should be fair and remember that these people are using their cells only for dire emergencies. Like the conversation I listened to on the downtown Broadway bus on route to having lunch with my mother.

"Oh! Thank goodness I got you! I'm just three blocks away! Tell me again the list . . . Milk! Bread! Cereal and—that's it! Cat food! I would have forgotten it. I'm one block away . . . Okay! If there's anything else we need, call me while I'm in the market! Either way, I'll call you as I'm leaving the market! See you in ten! Bye!"

Spare us, please. Just then, my phone vibrated.

"Hello?" I whispered.

Lo and behold, it was my mother. The bus came to an unexpected and abrupt stop, causing all of us who were standing to lurch forward.

"I can't hear you, Curtis."

I was stuck standing in the center section of an accordion bus. She ordered me to speak up, but the bus accelerated and twisted around a parked garbage truck, I was thrown off balance by the central pivot. My cell phone flew out of my hand and wedged itself into the rubber accordion flaps. I could hear my mother's voice squawking on the other end.

When I finally reached the phone I heard her scream, "Speak up!"

"I'm on the bus," I told her, out of breath, "and I don't want people hearing my conversation."

"No one cares what you have to say."

I couldn't believe she said that.

She informed me that there was a slight change of plans and that I was to meet them at the northwest corner of 56th Street and Seventh Avenue. She said "us," so I asked her if other people were joining us.

"There's someone I want you to meet," she said mischievously.

"Mother, we've been down this road so many times before. Just face it, Dolly Levy you're not."

"You'll like Robbie."

I'm sure this poor victim's name is Rob, but whenever possible my mother has the most annoying habit of immediately nicking a person's name by adding a y or an ie.

"And I've arranged it so the three of us can spend the entire afternoon together."

"You *what*?" I shot back. Every head on the bus turned to look at me, and I couldn't have cared less.

"Darling, my cell is breaking up."

Click. She hung up. Her cell is breaking up, my ass. I had twenty more blocks to stew over this sudden blind date.

I knew I shouldn't have told her about Dr. Tunick's plan to help me find a man. *Why do I feel compelled to tell her everything that is going on in my life?*

Like the day I told her that my doctor found out that my male hormones were way below the lowest acceptable level and that I now had to receive deep, painful hypodermic testosterone injections once a week in my butt. I limped for two days, feeling like someone had kicked me in the ass with a metal boot.

"So that explains your high-pitched voice, lack of facial hair, and attractive but boyish figure."

I corrected her. "Women have figures; I have a physique."

"Whatever. Now that you are hormonally normal, are you attracted to women?"

I just shook my head.

Distracted, I got off the bus too soon, at 59th Street. Maybe it was a good thing, giving me time to prepare for who knows what.

An arranged setup by my mother. *Who does she think she is, my pimp? Besides, she's hasn't a clue as to what I'm attracted to.*

And I can't spend the entire afternoon with them. It amazes me that people think that when you're a writer, you've got all this free time on your hands, that my day is totally flexible and on a moment's notice I can make a detour, stray from my very structured writing schedule, and take an afternoon off.

Just then I passed a poster advertising a Truffaut film festival downtown and my favorite of all favorites, *The Story Of Adele H.*, starring Isabelle Adjani, was playing. Maybe I could make the three o'clock showing?

As I approached 56th Street, I wondered why the change of address. What restaurant could we possibly be going to? Maybe it was The Russian Tea Room? But that's on 57th Street. Or La Caravelle? Then I sadly remembered that they'd closed. What was on the corner of Seventh and 56th?

I spotted my mother. She was facing uptown and talking very animatedly to Rob, whose back was to me. And it was a very nice back, I might add. He had tremendous lats and traps, thick, light-brown hair that was short but not too short, and plenty of it. He was wearing a polo shirt and casual slacks. If the front was as good as the back, maybe this wasn't going to be so bad after all.

Just steps away from them, what happened next stopped me dead in my tracks. I thought my mother was about to wave to me, but instead she wrapped one arm around that hunk's thick wrestler's neck, the other around his sculpted back. She ran her fingers through his hair and as I took a step closer, I saw that she was kissing him. And I don't mean a peck on the cheek. She was sucking face. My mother was inhaling Rob, my date, down her throat.

"Mother!" I cried.

She pulled away from Rob, and instead of looking guilty, like the cat that swallowed the canary, she had this huge, shit-eating grin on her face.

And then Rob turned around.

He . . . was a she!

I can't imagine the expression on my face.

"Close your mouth, dear, and say hello to Robbie."

I couldn't speak.

"I apologize for Curtis's bad manners." Then she pulled me aside. "What's your problem?"

I found my voice.

"You were just kissing a woman?"

"And your point is?" She pinched me really hard on my arm. "Snap out of it and say hello to her."

Robbie held out her large, masculine—I mean lesbian—hand and nearly shook my arm off.

"Nice to meet ya, Curtis. Your mother's been telling me all about your illustrious writing career." She winked at my mother and slapped me on the back, practically knocking a lung out. "She's proud of you winning all those special awards."

"Mother? Awards?" I asked under my breath. "What awards?"

Changing the subject as quickly as she could, she slipped one arm through mine and one through Robbie's. She then declared that she was famished and that over lunch they'd tell me all about how they met.

My mother swung us around like precision-perfect Radio City Rockettes and marched us forward till we came to an abrupt stop mid-block on West 56th Street.

"Here we are," she uttered with delight.

I know my jaw dropped even farther this time. I was staring at Hooters. Never in my life did I ever think I would enter this restaurant, let alone with my mother and her lesbian girlfriend.

Inside, it was full of businessmen on lunch breaks and mammary-enhanced waitresses. Ours in particular was so large that I swear her bra had to be reinforced with flying buttresses.

"Hi y'all. I'm Deb, and I'll be your Hooter gal for today," she said, handing out the menus. "So nice to see women in here for a change."

She bent over to wipe our table, nearly spilling out her pendulous breasts. Both my mother and her friend got a close-up view and then smiled at each other.

"Hi, Debbie," nicked my mother. "I'm starving. Robbie and I are going to split an order of nachos, and we're each having a bacon cheeseburger, well done."

"And a pitcher of beer," added the lesbian.

"And my son will have?"

"This one's your son?"

Dear God, what awful thing did I do in a past life to deserve this?

Deb continued. "Why, the two of you look more like brother and sister."

I wasn't sure if she was complimenting my mother or insulting me.

"Debbie, aren't you just the cutest little old thing?" my mother said. "What do you want, Curtis?"

"To be swallowed up into a black hole." She kicked me under the table. I yelped and said, "I'll have a manhattan straight up with Maker's Mark."

My mother gave me a look that could kill. "You've got to have more than that, darling."

"I'll have two manhattans straight up with Maker's Mark."

Deb said she'd be back in a jiffy with our drinks, and Robbie got up to go to the ladies' room. She kissed my mother in front of me and warned us not to talk about her while she was gone. I watched her as she sailed off, ogling all the hooters.

"Isn't she just great?" my mother gushed with pride. "She drives a tractor trailer for a living, and she smokes cigars."

"Mother, what's going on here?"

"I used the Tunick Technique."

"The what?"

"Darling, your shrink's way of finding a mate and—*poof*—Robbie appeared."

I slammed my fist on the table and declared that that was *my* technique and that Magda had prescribed it just for me. I didn't care *how* childish I sounded, and then I warned her of what the doctor said. One had to be very careful what one asked for.

"Curtis, I was very specific and I got just what I wanted." A smile exploded across her face. "A really nice girlfriend."

"But you can't be a lesbian," I whispered. "You're my mother."

She went on to criticize my narrow-mindedness. I was totally at a loss.

"Darling, before I met your father, I had a girlfriend. Don't get me wrong, I like men, and they're certainly necessary to procreate. But the only lovers who have ever understood me have been women."

"You mean you've had more than one?"

"Many."

I truly thought I was going to throw up. I searched my mind for something to grasp on to. I wanted to know how she could do this to my father and to his memory.

"Most of my memories of your father are not fond ones, Curtis. And besides, he died over fourteen years ago."

"But you never told me you were bisexual."

"Maybe it wasn't any of your business." My mother sat up taller as Robbie made her way back to the table. "Dear, haven't you heard of something called boundaries?"

ELEVEN

SQUATTER'S RIGHTS

Ten years ago, who would have thought that computers would become so indispensable to our lives? Each year—no, each month—a newfangled product comes out on the market. My favorite new toy is the almost-perfected Web camera.

When we're both online at the same time, it's wonderful to see Quinn's big head on my computer monitor. And with microphones and speakers, we can chat hands-free.

"Quinn, my mother is a lesbian."

He disappeared out of view of from his camera. I knew he'd have the same reaction that I did. He must have fallen off of his chair and onto the floor.

He reappeared with his shirt off and seemed to be laughing. I asked him if he had heard what I said.

"Duh."

Quinn's image freeze-framed, flickered, and then he was live again.

"I think there's something wrong with our connection, Quinn, because I think I just heard you say 'duh.' "

He was laughing harder. "I did just say 'duh,' because I know that. She's told everyone about her lesbian lovers."

I was dumbfounded.

"Why the hell would she tell you and not me?"

When camming, you can see your own image in a box on your computer screen, and at that moment, I panicked at how scrunched up my face was. I could hear my mother's voice saying *Don't make that face—it will stay that way.*

"Maybe she thinks you'll judge her?"

"The thought of her being with another woman is just so . . . gross."

Quinn shook his head disapprovingly.

"She used the Tunick Technique, as she's dubbed it, and is now dating this really butch dyke."

Quinn squirmed on his seat. "How is it working for *you?*"

"Nil, and I don't know where to look next."

He bent over, out of frame. "Why don't you go to The Town-crier?"

What the hell was he doing? "Quinn, that's a wrinkle bar."

He popped back up into view. "And how old are you, Curtis?"

But I'm not wrinkled. I looked at my face closely on my monitor. I couldn't be. I've been drinking Oil of Delay for twenty years.

Quinn bent over and out of view again. "If you're truly look-ing to meet men of substance who are stable and secure, go to The Towncrier."

"I'll go there over my dead body."

Actually, The Towncrier is a gay bar decked out like a funeral parlor. There's an overabundance of flowers, Naugahyde love seats, and walls covered in green-and-red plaid wallpaper. And the piano is tucked away in an alcove where the open casket should be. Not to mention that everyone who goes there is dressed in black. They look like either morticians or walking cadavers.

"Curtis, I give up. You ask for my advice, and when I give it, you just shoot it down. I have to jump in the shower and then go pick up my car at the garage."

It turns out that Quinn had gotten caught up in a bit of gunfire. He cut a guy off on the Pasadena Freeway, which really pissed him off. Shortly after that, the other driver caught up to Quinn and started playing cat and mouse with him. He even swerved dangerously close, trying to sideswipe him. Quinn gave him the finger, hit the gas, and sped off. When the guy caught up to him again, he pulled out a gun and shot a bullet right through Quinn's rear window. It just missed him, exiting through the front windshield.

"Do you know how fucking expensive two windshields are?"

I was shocked, to say the least. "That's so awful, so incredible, so . . . so—"

"So road rage?"

And people think New York City is unsafe.

"Curtis, go to The Towncrier, and I want a full report in the morning."

"Drive safe, and keep your finger to yourself," I warned him.

"Okay. Going to take a shower."

Just then, he stood up stark naked and walked off to the bathroom. Oh, the wonders of the twenty-first century. That was way too much visual information.

≳ ≲

If I'm going to a wrinkle bar, I'm going to look my best, and that means showing off the 270 deep squats that I do each week to keep this middle-aged white man's butt pointing north. Hence, I slipped into my snug black 501s, which are casual and sexy and create a false basket, thank you very much, and put on a white cotton V-neck short-sleeve shirt to accentuate the triceps and biceps that I've painfully sculpted, and I was armed.

As I approached the somber-looking façade of The Towncrier, a funeral director-like character pulled open the front door and welcomed me with some sort of mumble.

Upon entering, I did what I always do in these environments,

I quickly scurried to the first opening at the bar. Keeping my back to the audience in order to show off my best asset, I caught the bartender's eye and ordered my usual.

One sip of mother's milk and I slowly turned around to scour the crowd. All I could see was a wake of gray suits, gray ties, gray hair, and gray skin. *What am I doing?* I turned around to take another sip of my drink.

"Is that a cosmopolitan?" boomed a thick, throaty bass voice.

I turned and noticed the man next to me for the first time. At eye level I saw the most incredible pair of pectoral muscles aching to burst out of a skintight black t-shirt. I looked up this wall of muscle to his face and nearly keeled over.

"No, it's not a cosmopolitan," I squeaked. "It's a manhattan."

Thank you, Quinn. Thank you for recommending The Towncrier. Already I could picture the two of us living happily ever after.

"Curtis here."

"J.R."

He wanted me. I could tell this man wanted me.

"Curtis?"

"Yes, J.R.?"

He looked me straight in the eye. "Now that you have your manhattan, leave this bar."

"I beg your pardon?"

He warned me that this didn't have to get ugly, and again asked me to leave the bar. Not The Towncrier, but the front bar. He suggested that I go to the back bar or the bar downstairs.

What was going on here? What does he do, own the front bar?

"I'm not moving," I said emphatically.

J.R. took a deep breath and looked around the room before addressing me again. "We're both working tonight. You respect my space, and I'll respect yours. The front bar is mine." With a very erect index finger, he poked me in the chest. "Now beat it."

It suddenly dawned on me. "You're a hustler?"

He shushed me. "Keep it down, man. What's wrong with you? You want to get us both thrown out of here?"

I was so happy he thought I was a hooker. I *knew* I wasn't too old. Wait a minute—was that an insult? A middle-aged prostitute? Who would have thought?

He commented on how I was dressed and how he was dressed. And then he pointed out how all the other men were dressed and how they were looking at how we were dressed.

J.R. was right. I was mortified. These hungry-looking, double-breasted, testosterone-deprived octogenarians were eyeing me like a piece of beef. A priceless piece of beef, mind you.

I thought for a moment and then turned to J.R.

"I'm not a call boy, I'm a writer." I paused. "How much do you charge?"

"You buying?"

"Maybe?"

"Two hundred fifty dollars."

"What do I get for that?"

He informed me that I get all twelve inches of J.R. What was I going to do with twelve inches? Dress it up and play house with it?

I passed on the offer. I haven't sunk so low that I have to pay for it . . . yet.

"Then step aside, boy," J.R. said, giving me a look like he was going to crush me.

And with that, I gracefully picked up my manhattan and, stepping and sipping, proceeded to the back bar. I knew I was heading in the right direction, because I could hear the voice of a tired old queen warbling out one more rendition of "The Trolley Song."

I entered the room and stood at the doorway. And in the

far corner, believe it or not, there it was, the ever-popular baby grand piano surrounded by, or should I say supporting a handful of, silver-haired foxes.

To my left I heard a gasp. To my right, "Fresh meat," followed by the sound of cold wrinkled cash being pulled out of Brooks Brothers pants pockets.

"Are you working tonight, son?" asked an elderly man who was a dead ringer, vocally, for Katharine Hepburn.

"No, pops," I said as I headed to the piano.

Just drink your drink and leave, Curtis. I nestled in between two men.

"You hairless all over?" asked one who was literally dribbling into his scotch.

"Am I *what?*"

"I asked if you were hairless, you know, down there between your legs?"

As I quickly got up and moved diagonally across the room to a love seat, I felt scores of cataract-infested eyes desperately searching for a clearer image of me.

I took a seat and gulped my drink.

"Anyone sitting here?" asked an exotic-looking man of maybe thirty with what sounded like a deep Russian accent. He, too, was wearing a T-shirt and jeans.

"I don't think so," I replied, offering him the seat next to me. "You working tonight?"

We both laughed while his round, softball-sized biceps curled as he took a swig of his beer.

There was an uncomfortable lull in our conversation as a man slowly shuffled by with a walker, reeking of mothballs.

"Someday that will be us," the Russian declared.

"Speak for yourself," I cried. "Club me first."

Just then, the club's bartender clubbed the Russian.

"Buddy, you forgot to pay for your beer," he said, looking at my new friend.

"Really?" he said, reaching into his pocket. He looked at his money and then at me.

"Dude, can you cover this?" he asked, never really showing me the money. "All I have are large bills."

Awkwardly put on the spot, I pulled out a five and told the bartender to keep the change.

"Thanks for the beer, man." He looked me up and down. "Are you hungry?"

Was that a set-up for a punch line, or was he seriously asking me if I was hungry for food?

Either way, I said, "I'm starving." And with that, we left The Towncrier.

Once outside, we both took a deep breath of fresh air, and that's when I noticed that he had the most incredible butt I had ever seen in my life. I had to ask him what type of squats he did. He not only told me, he demonstrated them for me right there on the street.

He did squats with feet parallel to his shoulders, squats with his feet wide apart, and squats with his feet close together. I asked him if he could show me the squats with his legs wide apart again. He obliged, and I thought I was going to faint.

On top of that, he said he taught spinning. I was thinking that if I had his two ripe melons in front of me for motivation, I could cycle through eternity. This was my man. I just needed to find out his name first.

"Park," he said.

"Bark?"

"No, my name is Park." He laughed. "As in Parker."

"And mine is Curtis." I made a funny face. "Parker? I assumed you were Russian?"

He said he was born Yevgeniy Gurevich. How exciting, my first Russian Jew. He Americanized his name to Park to fit in easier. He should have picked Bob, I thought, as we headed toward Third Avenue for dinner.

≳ ≲

"I love lobster, hate lima beans," I declared as Park nursed his cosmopolitan.

I could eat lobster morning, noon, and night. In fact, on my last trip to Provincetown, I had some sort of lobster for lunch and dinner every day.

But God forbid I have to cook one at home. I could never boil something to death. I swear my mother delighted in the screams for help we could hear from the lobsters she would cook, but I'm too chicken. Speaking of which, if I had to kill a chicken, or a lamb, or a pig, or a cow or its baby calf, I'd be a vegetarian. I'm a hypocritical butchering wimp, but at least I admit it.

At that moment, Park's eyes got really squinty. I stared at him, and then his eyes popped wide open. Thinking it was the alcohol, I suggested that he order some food.

"No, Curtis, I'll just pick from your plate."

Like hell he will.

"Waiter?" I laughed off how serious I was. I don't share my lobster with anyone.

He appeared.

"I'd like to change my order. Let's make it a double order of lobster. I feel like splurging."

Both the waiter and I looked over at Park. He was sitting upright and facing me, but his eyes were shut.

"Park?" I whispered.

"Bark?" asked the waiter.

"No, Park, as in Parker." But he didn't move. His eyes didn't open.

"Park?" asked the waiter.

What was wrong? He was obviously breathing. Had he passed out? Was he hypoglycemic or diabetic or even epileptic?

And suddenly Park's eyes burst open. Incredulous, the waiter and I just stared at him.

"What?" asked Park.

"You just zoned out," I said.

He confessed to having had a really long day and hoped he could take a rain check. He had an early-morning class to teach and wanted to hit the sack.

I stood up to say good-bye.

"I'll make it up to you," he promised. "Can you cover my drink?"

My little red flag went up.

"And how about dinner at my place later this week? Call me. Park Trice."

The waiter and I looked at each other.

"I'm in the book."

The waiter was still standing by my side as we watched him exit the restaurant.

"That was pretty weird," he whispered.

"You can say that again," I agreed as I sat back down at the table.

"But great buns." He cleared Park's place away. "Are you going to call him?"

I sipped my drink. "Hell, yes."

"Are you going to stay?"

I buttered a roll. "Hell, yes."

"Are you still going to have the lobster?"

"Hell yes," I said as I tied the bib around my neck. "I want both of them."

≳ ≲

The Russian lived on Ann Street in Manhattan. I had never heard of Ann Street, so I did a MapQuest search on the Internet to see where it was and lo and behold, there was Ann

Street, south of the Brooklyn Bridge.

Park gave me subway directions from the Upper West Side, and I allowed forty-five minutes to get to his place. I had to take a train downtown from 96th and Broadway to an A train at 59th Street. I rode that to West 4th Street, where I had to transfer to the F train. The F would take me to the 6, and I had to stay on that till I got to the City Hall Park stop. I was forty minutes late and swore I would take a cab home even if it cost $100. This was akin to taking a slow boat to Siberia.

Once outside his apartment, I gave Quinn a quick call and caught him on his way into the beauty parlor.

"You're seeing who?" I asked.

He was out of breath. "My cosmetician."

Quinn took to dying his eyelashes in order to keep up with his Day-Glo green contact lenses. He said this woman was the best in Hollywood, but if you were late, she'd drop you like a hot potato and would advance to her next client. And getting appointments was tough because she was booked months in advance. I'm in the wrong profession.

"Curtis, what's that clicking sound?" Quinn asked as he literally ran to her studio.

I aimed my new digital camera at Parker's apartment building and took another picture.

"I'm playing with my new toy."

Quinn must have been shoving people right and left, considering the cursing I heard in the background. "What's his name?"

I hesitated for a moment. "Park Trice."

"Bark Twice?"

"Parker Trice, and be nice," I said, knowing he was going to do that.

He warned me that I was setting myself up for yet another disappointment.

I snapped another picture. "Quinn, to tell you the truth, all

I want is a taste of his buns. Nothing more."

I've become so primal. Okay, trampy is more like it.

Quinn wanted his phone number just in case he didn't hear back from me. He felt it would give the cops a clue as to which river to dredge my body from.

I heard wrestling and then, "Out of that chair, bitch." Someone fell to the ground as Quinn plopped down in the seat. "It's my appointment."

I closed the phone, threw it into my pocket, took a deep breath, and pressed the buzzer for apartment number three.

It was a walk-up tenement with a stone relief at the top of the building that displayed the year 1858. His apartment must be on the first or second floor. Six flights later I reached his floor, checking for a nosebleed.

Park was standing in his doorway, wearing bicycle shorts and a tank top, which took away what little breath I had left in me.

"Since when is apartment three on the sixth floor?" I asked.

"Sorry, I should have warned you."

"Now I know how you keep those buns in shape."

He laughed, inviting me in. As he turned around and entered the apartment the light gray material of his shorts hugged his gluts and slid up his crack just enough to make my knees buckle beneath me.

I walked into his apartment, and it was virtually empty. He referred to himself as a Spartan hedonist with minimalist tendencies, with a few choice things of great value and sentiment. I understood the Spartan and minimalist concept, but where were the few choice things?

He even had a tub in the kitchen. Originally, these apartments were called cold-water flats. They still were, except that nowadays they had hot water. I hoped.

"The bathroom's in the outside hall," he added. "My rent is hardly anything."

I would hope so.

"I have dinner all ready. You hungry?" he asked as he turned his back to me to get something out of the fridge.

"Famished," I said, salivating at his backside.

I took a seat on the lower-than-I-expected futon and did a half gainer onto my back. Luckily, he was getting me a beer and didn't notice. I jumped into a conversation and told him I was worried about the other night.

"I'm sorry, Curtis, I should have told you that I'm narcoleptic."

I touched my wallet. "You steal things?"

"No," he laughed. "I fall asleep at a moment's notice."

I nodded as though I had known that all along.

Park said that sometimes he knew when it was going to happen and sometimes he didn't. Stress definitely played a factor. It's so bad he can't even drive a car.

Concerned, I asked, "Is there a pill you can take or something?"

"You'd think caffeine would help, but nothing works."

I thought that that was really horrible as he brought beers over and a plate of bread and cheese, which he placed in front of me on the floor. We toasted to stress-free living, and he responded with something in Russian. We clinked beer bottles, and then Park brought another plate and silverware in from the kitchen.

He sat down next to me and placed the second dish in front of himself. On it was half of a roasted chicken, steamed brussels sprouts, dilled carrots, and wild rice with mushrooms.

"Bon appétit," Park said as he slipped his napkin under his chin and picked up his knife and fork.

I looked at his overflowing plate of mouthwatering food and then I looked at my plate of bread and cheese. Then I looked back at his.

"Park?"

He started to inhale his dinner. Inhale is too tame and much too polite. He began shoveling his food into his mouth. I wanted to tell him to take human bites.

"Why do I get the plate of bread and cheese and you get the roasted chicken and vegetables?"

"Not enough for two?" he garbled.

"I see."

What I saw clearly was that Park was cheap. Like a mouse, I picked at my cheese and nibbled at my bread.

As I wondered what I had gotten myself into and why I was even there, Park quickly reminded me.

"Salt!" he shouted as he jumped to his feet and strutted to the kitchen. The sheer beauty of his backside was reason enough to stay.

Dinner lasted all of seven-and-a-half minutes. Park picked up his plate and carried it over to the sink.

Sated, he then stretched his body while walking down the hallway to his bedroom. I brought my full plate of bread and cheese into the kitchen and ran to catch up to him. Maybe this evening wasn't going to be a disaster after all.

The only other things in the room were a television and a small dresser. He threw himself down on the bed and pointed to the closet.

"Take a look at the videos and let me know what you'd like to watch."

I guess videos were on the menu? I looked into the closet and my eyes went right to it, *Buns of Steel*.

"So, Park? Is this a good workout tape?" I asked, handing the video to him.

"Excellent. Let me show you."

He slipped in the video as I slipped onto his bed.

Park promptly took off his shirt, revealing a rock-hard torso; climbed onto the bed; and proceeded to get on all fours and do butt exercises along with the almost-as-hot-and-sexy video model.

"See, the key is to engage the glutes without cheating with the hip flexors, lower back, or hamstring. It's tough to isolate. Helps if someone creates resistance. Can you create resistance, Curtis, by pressing down on my foot as I push up and away?"

I was mesmerized and speechless by the contracting action of his ass.

"Curtis?"

"What?"

"I asked if you could resist."

"No, no, I can't," I said, out of breath.

And with that, I jumped him. And he seemed very happy to be jumped. But no matter how much I wanted his butt, the correct and proper side of me knew I should kiss him first.

Damn, even his kisses felt stingy. His lips were tight and pursed, occasionally letting out a snakelike darting of his tongue. I hate bad kissers. But his rear was worth it.

We rolled around a bit until I found myself underneath him.

"Hope I look as good as you do when I'm your age, Curtis," he said as he started some sort of grinding action with his pelvis.

"Please, Park, let's dispense with the romantic talk."

The grinding turned into a rather irritating dry hump, so I tried to wrestle him off me.

"You're hot for an old guy. And strong."

That having ticked me off, I really started to wrestle, causing his shorts to slip down around his ankles. Park stopped and looked deeply into my eyes.

"But don't forget to leave the money on the dresser."

Mortified and fearing that I had heard him correctly, I stopped resisting as he started that damn pelvis action again.

Just then, his less-than-sexy grinding came to a grinding halt. There was a split second before Park's entire body released its full dead weight upon me.

"Park?" I whispered.

He didn't respond.

"Park," I said a bit louder.

Again, he didn't respond.

"Park, get off of me!"

He was out, dead to the world.

I managed to squeeze out from underneath him as he let out a deep snore. I sat on the edge of the bed to gather my thoughts and then glanced over at the *Buns of Steel* video. I got up, switched it off, and looked over at Park lying on his stomach, his exposed derriere pointing up to the heavens.

What a waste of a beautiful body part. What a waste of my time. Leave the money on the dresser? I laughed.

I went into the living room and grabbed my coat and digital camera. I was heading for the front door and then stopped dead in my tracks. It didn't have to be a total waste of my time.

I tiptoed back into the bedroom and stood at the doorway, making sure Park was still asleep. One huge roar of a snore confirmed that the coast was clear.

I walked over to him. The excitement at seeing his bare bottom, coupled with the sheer debauchery of what I was about to do, literally made me tremble as I held up the camera. With the ease of a seasoned *National Geographic* photographer knowing he had one shot to get the picture of a lifetime, I focused in on his luscious behind and clicked.

The shutter release stirred Park from his deep sleep, and in a flash I was out the front door.

I had to call Quinn in LA immediately.

"I can't talk, my lashes are drying," he mumbled through clenched teeth.

"What did she do, give you a root canal while she was at it?" I filled him in on the brief but exciting evening as I tried to hail a cab.

"Narcoleptic?" he asked. "Isn't that someone who sleeps

with dead people?"

One cab with passengers passed me. "Honestly, Quinn, you're Mr. Malapropism. He can't stay awake." I walked to the intersection of Ann and William, hoping I'd do better.

"Curtis, do you feel guilty about what you did?"

An available taxi drove right by me, even though my arms were flailing. "Hell, yes."

"Was Park a hustler?"

It was a wasteland, as I looked west down Ann Street. No cabs at all. "Hell, yes."

"Do you feel you had a right to do what you did?" Quinn asked, laughing.

I stopped. "Hell, yes. I have squatter's rights."

"Good. E-mail me the picture."

I trudged to the subway.

TWELVE

DEHALF-WITT

The last place I ever thought I would end up at was Hooters. The second-to-last place was a lesbian softball game. But I did want to support my mother as she supported Robbie.

Central Park has a pair of ball fields just south of the West 66th Street entrance. Each diamond had recently been refurbished with a new truckload of fresh sand; plush, green sod; and a few rows of stands for spectators. But the best part is that it's located next to the merry-go-round.

With a combination of the warm sun, the oversized pretzel with mustard, the cheering of the ballplayers, and the music from the carousel, it all felt quite movielike. What kind of movie I'm not sure, but it did feel special.

I was trying to share the moment with Quinn, but I still hadn't gotten the hang of text messaging with my cell phone. He was in the middle of taping a show and couldn't talk, so he was messaging back from a computer. I'm used to typing on a keyboard, but I found that punching in words on this tiny pad was maddening, to say the least.

While finishing a cryptic sentence telling Quinn that I had placed a personal ad in a few gay publications, I heard the smack of a softball against a bat, a roar from the crowd, and then air whooshing by my right ear.

The female umpire screamed foul as I said a prayer. I'm frightened to death of small flying objects, and this one just missed me. My mother was sitting next to me on the sidelines, a one-woman cheerleading squad. At that moment she stood up and did another cheer. It looked like she was doing a spastic version of the Swim. Think jiggling butt and shaking arms.

"Shiny as a Cadillac, shifting gear to gear! We're the Westchester Lesbians, and here's our cheer! Fight! Fight! Fight that other team! Fight! Fight! Fight that other team! Fight! Fight! Fight that other team! Goooooooooo Robbie!"

And Robbie hollered back from home plate, "Love ya!"

Robbie was playing catcher. What she had caught was my mother.

Quinn's message popped up: ". . . don't hate me . . . used Tunick Technique . . . met a great guy."

I couldn't believe it. It's just so perfect. Quinn and my mother were matched up, and here I was, Miss Lonely Hearts, writing and responding to pathetic ads in *The Village Voice*.

I took a deep breath and typed a message describing a guy I was going to meet. "GBM, banker, 5'10", 175 lbs. Bald with goatee seeks GWM between the ages of 20 and 50 who has just as much between his ears as he does between his legs."

I waited for his response.

He wrote, "Too vague . . . relax."

I slammed the phone shut. I can't relax—I'm desperate. I'm a desperate man. I wondered if I was trying too hard. What if I stopped looking? Maybe then I would collide into my soul mate. But I'm forty-five fucking years old. What if we don't clunk heads until I'm eighty? And who's talking about a soul mate? I'll settle for a gorgeous, smart, funny, sexy, wealthy, sensitive man who wants a long-term monogamous relationship and adores me.

"That's a simple order," my mother said.

She pulled me out of my inner dialogue. Actually, my outer dialogue, since I was speaking out loud to myself.

"Are you really looking for a lover, or just notches in your belt?" she asked me.

I looked at her with shock. "You and Quinn are having way more sex than I am."

My phone vibrated and it was Quinn. He didn't even wait for me to say hello.

"Curtis, you're getting more uptight and rigid every day."

I felt as though the two of them were ganging up on me. "I'm extremely flexible and easygoing."

"You are not flexible," my mother chimed in.

"I can still do my splits."

"Nor easygoing," Quinn added. "Curtis, you have so many guidelines, so many rules that guys have to follow."

Those are standards, I thought to myself.

Quinn continued. "Granted, you demand just as much from yourself, but what you're looking for just doesn't exist."

"But I exist."

"Then fuck yourself," he said.

Quinn and I were both silent for a moment and then burst out into laughter.

"Curtis," he said, "lower your standards. You'll have a lot more fun. Gotta run, sweetie. Colt is meeting me at the studio."

"Colt? What is he, a horse?"

"No, but he's hung like one."

Now *that* made me smile.

"Curtis, where are you meeting this guy?"

"Barnes and Noble. He said he'll be wearing a plaid flannel work shirt, and he's been wearing them since way before they were hip and cool."

"Good luck, Curtis. I'll be here to pick up the pieces."

I hung up my cell phone just in time for that small flying object to hit me right on the left cheek.

The initial impact made me see stars, and then the unbearable pain started. The ball bounced off my face and right into my mother's hands.

"I caught it!" she screamed. "I caught it!" She bolted to her feet. "Is she out? Is she out?"

"She's been out for ages," yelled Robbie.

Team members cheered as the umpire hollered, "Foul ball!"

"Oh, no!" I cried as I felt my cheek swelling.

"I agree dear," she said as she made the out signal with her arms. "It should be an out."

I touched my cheek. "Mother, that ball just hit me right in the face."

She shook her finger at me. "Well, Chatty Cathy, if you were watching the game instead of talking on the phone—"

I cut her off with a look that told her not to *even* go there. "It's enough that I showed up, Mother."

"And I thank you, Curtis," she said as she kissed my throbbing face. "It means a great deal to Robbie and me. I think you're going to be seeing a lot of her."

Did this mean the two of them were getting serious?

"Look," she said as she proudly held out a small silver object. "A gift from Robbie. Read the inscription."

"To my lipstick lesbo, love Robbie." I looked at my mother. "Lipstick lesbo?"

"That's what she calls me. Well, I've shortened it to Lippy."

Lippy the Lesbo. I took a deep breath and put the ice from my soft drink onto my cheek.

"She's just so beautiful, Curtis. We woke up together this morning, and I shared with her my self-consciousness about having gained a little weight, and she said, 'Don't you dare lose a pound, Lippy. I love every ounce of you, just the way you are.' And then she made love to me again, whispering into my ear, 'Fat is a lesbian issue.' "

I didn't even want her to explain that one to me.

"Batter up!" hollered the umpire.

I'm not sure which was making me dizzier, the softball that

hit me in the head or the thought of my mother having sex with another woman.

As the ballplayer swung the bat a few times, Robbie hollered, "Ya can't hit the broad side of a barn."

The pitcher wound up and threw the ball, and the batter swung. She may not be able to hit the broad side of a barn, but she certainly hit the lesbian side of a broad. She fouled the ball straight back into Robbie's gut. Her catcher's gear absorbed most of the shock but still knocked her off her feet and onto her butt.

The other team roared with laughter as my mother ran to her side. Something inside of Robbie snapped, and in a flash she was on top of the batter, knocking the shit out of her.

I pulled my mother away for fear that she would get hurt, and we watched as it took four team members to pull Robbie off the girl. She was definitely way out of control.

"You fucking hit me on purpose," Robbie screamed. "I'm going to kill your fucking ass, you fucking asshole."

The teammates released their grips, and she jumped the player, punching her in the stomach.

Again, the team pulled Robbie off her as the umpire hollered, "You're outta the game."

"Fuck you!" Robbie shrieked. "Fuck you all!"

My mother went to her side. "There, there, Robbie. It's only a game," my mother soothed as she slid her arm into hers.

"Don't fucking touch me!" Robbie shouted as she pulled her arm away.

And with that, Robbie stormed off the field.

My mother and I were silent. She was clearly shaken up.

"You going to be okay, Mother?"

She nodded. I offered to find her a cab, but she declined.

"I'm going to catch up with Robbie," she said as she dusted herself off. "Her temper cools down pretty fast."

"Maybe you should leave her alone."

"Don't be such a worrywart." She kissed me good-bye. "I can take care of myself."

I looked at my watch.

"Where are you off to?"

"A blind date."

"You're a bigger man than I," she said as she embraced me.

I wasn't so sure of that, as I watched her wave good-bye and trail after Robbie.

≥ ≤

Heart pounding, palms sweaty, and cheek swollen, I entered Barnes & Noble a few minutes early and strategically planted myself in the magazine section. This way I'd be able to see him before he saw me. I grabbed a copy of *Ebony* and waited.

A bald black man with a goatee entered the store, but I couldn't see what kind of shirt he had on. He looked around and then walked right toward me. I was just about to say hello when he passed me. Thank goodness—his head was too pointy.

Out of the corner of my eye, I noticed the security guard checking me out. Another bald black man with a goatee entered the store and started walking toward me. He was wearing a plaid shirt and had a huge smile on his face. He came closer, and closer and just when I was about to put out my hand to shake, he passed me by for a woman standing behind me. Thank goodness—he was too fat. I didn't know there were so many bald black men with goatees in New York City.

Glancing at my watch and furious that he was one minute late, I looked up and the security guard was making his way toward me. He was a bald black man with a goatee, and easy on the eyes. Maybe this was Rudolph.

"Sir?" he asked.

I smiled, extending my hand.

He grabbed my elbow. "You're going to have to leave the store."

"But aren't you—"

"Sir," he said as he escorted me to the front door, "the management reserves the right to ask anyone acting suspiciously to leave the store."

"Suspiciously?" I pulled away from him. "You think I'm acting suspiciously?"

"Then what are you doing, sir?"

"I'm waiting for my friend, Rudolph."

"Curtis?" A gorgeous bald black man with a goatee and plaid flannel work shirt that he'd been wearing since way before it was hip and gay stepped forward. "I'm Rudolph."

"Yes," I said, pointing to him, "this is my Rudolph. See?" I quickly rushed him out of Barnes & Noble.

I caught my breath. "It's a pleasure to meet you, Rudolph." I looked at him again. "Man, you really are beautiful."

"Yes, I know," he said, flashing a smile. "I'm a beacon of light. Gay men are attracted to me like moths to a flame."

Healthy ego he's got there. Intuitively, I kept stroking. "I mean, never in my wildest dreams did I think that a blind date would turn out to be more handsome than I had expected— no, *hoped*— for."

"Babe, the feeling is mutual." He brushed the side of my face. "But what's wrong with your cheek?"

I covered it with my hand. "Something kind of hit it."

He examined it. "It's swollen up to the size of a softball."

Little did he know. He kissed it gently and then slipped his hand in mine, intertwining our fingers. It was an instant physical click.

He squeezed my hand. "I don't want to rush things or jump the gun, babe, but you're the one."

I thought, *If you're for real, Rudolph, you're not rushing. I've been waiting forty-five years for this.*

He gazed into my eyes. "I look at you and I know I have found the man I want to spend the next twenty years of my life with. What's your name again?"

Embarrassed, I looked away. "Curtis."

"Right, babe," he whispered, kissing my hand. "Let's toast with merlot."

Merlot? He rushed me to the end of the block and into a cab.

"Take us to Seventeenth and Eighth," he barked to the cabbie. "I had given up hope. Then I came across your personal and I thought, he's too good to be true."

He may be on to something there.

"Babe, we have the same interests." He looked out the window as his voice cracked. "We both believe in monogamy and are interested in a serious relationship and . . ."

At this point, my masculine strapping hunk of a man began to cry. For a minute few, this is a turn-on. For the rest of us, it's very uncomfortable.

He continued. "I knew my next lover would be HIV-positive, like I am."

I didn't know what to say. "Rudolph, that is so moving."

"Actually, my name is DeWitt."

I looked at him blankly.

"Till I know I can trust someone, I prefer to use a silly alias."

I looked more blankly. "Rudolph as opposed to DeWitt?"

He nodded, knowing how clever he was.

"Well, my name is still Curtis."

He kissed my hand again. "Right, babe."

"So, your name is DeWitt," I winked. "As in Addison?"

"No, as in North Babylon."

A gay man who hasn't seen *All About Eve?*

"That's where I grew up and live now. You've been out there?"

"Luckily, just in passing." I laughed, waiting for a response, but there was none.

"Here we are," DeWitt said as he jumped out of the cab.

I had a feeling of dread that I was going to waste a lot of good material on this guy.

"Babe, I wanted to take you to a quiet little gay restaurant where I can show you off."

I stepped out of the cab and looked at the restaurant. He brought me to The Food Trough?

"Only the best for my babe."

The Food Trough used to be a high-end establishment that attracted an upscale, mixed clientele and was especially enjoyable around the holidays. The same owners had downscaled it, turning it into a trendy gay eatery where straights loved to come and amusingly observe us. And the boys packed themselves in like sardines.

I barely squeezed into the crowed restaurant.

"Hey, Tony!" my escort shouted to the host.

"DeWitt." I guess he trusts Tony. "Your table's available." He smiled and gestured us to follow him.

"Tony, this is babe." He grabbed hold of my hand. "babe, this is Tony."

I tried to smile.

"Hi, babe."

I was beginning to feel like a pig. Appropriate that we're eating at The Food Trough. We were seated at the one table that could be seen by all other tables. DeWitt sat down as I attempted to sit across from him.

"No, babe," he said, pulling me toward him. "I like it European-style."

I held my tongue.

"Please," he said, "sit next to me on the banquette."

Due to an old gymnastic injury, I could feel my neck cramping up as he tried to sit me down to his right.

"DeWitt, I'm the opposite of Claudette Colbert." I flashed him my profile. "I only let people shoot me from the right."

"Claudette who?"

Another good one wasted. "Never mind. Can I sit on your left?"

"Babe, you can sit wherever you like," he whispered as he let me in first. There was a tablecloth, and on top of that was a sheet of white paper. Scooting across, I managed to paper cut the web of skin between the index and middle fingers of my left hand.

Thankfully, the din in the full restaurant drowned out my cry of pain. DeWitt seemed oblivious as to what happened even as I wrapped the bleeding hand in my napkin.

"Oh, waiter?" I called out as he passed by. I needed a drink.

"That's not just a waiter," DeWitt informed me. "You can call him Butler."

With him finally onto the *All About Eve* references, I said in my best Marilyn voice, "Well, I can't yell 'Oh, butler,' can I? Maybe somebody's name is Butler."

"His name *is* Butler," he said, totally straight.

DeWitt wasn't on to anything. This was going to be a long night.

"Would you like something to drink?" Butler asked.

I was just about to ask for my usual when DeWitt beat me to it.

"Merlot for two," he said, looking back down at his menu.

I glanced at him and then nodded okay to the waiter. I could feel the hangover already.

What was DeWitt doing, memorizing the menu? I just sat there as a busboy set a basket of bread and a dishful of olive oil down on the table along with a carton of crayons. There's nothing more obnoxious than people who doodle on paper-covered tables. All I've ever seen are scribbling of childlike stick figures.

Eventually, I broke the deafening silence and tried once more. "I noticed in my liquor store a wine called Marilyn Merlot." I waited for a response. The clock ticked by. "Get it, Marilyn Merlot, and they have her picture on the label?"

He finally looked up from his menu. "I want this to be the most extreme relationship."

Relationship? Extreme? I'm Mr. Jump The Gun, but this is ridiculous.

"Communication is key," he continued.

I nodded, and suddenly he started crying again. I mean really bawling. This large, bald black man with a goatee, plaid shirt, two earrings, who was better looking than The Rock was crying into the cold-pressed olive oil meant for dipping of focaccia bread.

He wiped away his tears. "I've always dreamt of meeting a man like you, babe."

I felt horribly self-conscious. "Gee, well, I'm flattered."

Butler reappeared with the merlot. Just looking at the deep red color was giving me a headache.

"We have only one special left tonight," the waiter informed us. "The calamari."

I hoped it was fried so that there was some sort of taste while disguising the tentacles.

"It's sautéed," he told us.

Not for me. "I'll have—"

"We'll have two orders of the squid," declared DeWitt.

"That makes my job easy." And off Butler went.

I looked at my date's neck and choked my wineglass.

"Here's to being open and honest," DeWitt toasted.

Hopefully I would be, I thought as we clinked glasses. And then his cell phone went off. Normally, I would have been offended if he answered it, but on this special occasion, I welcomed it.

"Hey Tawanda. 'Sup?"

I quickly scanned the room, which looked like a giant life raft of gay couplings clinging to each other, drowning in a sea of too much, too soon.

"Mama's smoking dope with Devan?"

I could relate to that.

"Send them both to their rooms and I'll talk to them tomorrow. Gotta go, I'm on a date." He looked over at me and blew a kiss. "Yea, she's beautiful, and hot, too."

I choked on some bread. Did he just say "she"?

"I'll come by in the morning." He hung up and swallowed a large mouthful of merlot.

I swallowed a larger one. "She? You referred to me as a she?"

He explained that he wasn't out to everyone and that his mother was smoking marijuana with Devan because it helps her glaucoma.

I nervously started folding and refolding the white paper that covered the table. "And who is Devan, and how does it help him?"

"It's only hurting Devan and his schoolwork. He's in eighth grade." DeWitt took a dramatic pause, grabbed my nonbandaged hand, and held on tightly. "Please don't reject me, and please don't run."

God, I wanted to run, but he was holding my hand too tightly.

"Devan is my son."

I looked at my glass of merlot, took a swig, and said, "I can handle that. So you have a son."

"I have two."

I took two sips of merlot and my glass was empty. "Oh, Butler," I said as the waiter went by. "Another merlot, and make it fast."

"His name is Evan, and he's in ninth grade."

Devan and Evan. "And do these boys have a mother?"

We looked at each other and simultaneously said, "Tawanda."

"My wife," he added.

I corrected him. "Your ex-wife."

He corrected me. "No, current wife."

I pulled out a pink crayon and started doodling. "Let me ask you something, DeWitt. Are you gay?"

"Of course, babe. I was bisexual till about four months ago, but now I'm strictly gay."

I drew a big, fat, straight line.

"But you're in the closet?" I added a large circle on top of it.

"Just to my family and close friends."

The people that matter the most, I thought. Uncontrollably, I drew short, stubby lines coming out of the center one. "So, you're still married to your wife?"

"Yes."

I drew circles on the ends of all the short lines. "And you're getting divorced?"

"No, why?"

"Because that would be the normal thing to do?" I drew curlicues on top of the big circle on top.

"There's nothing normal about me, babe."

I could see that. I scribbled three dots and a slash inside of the circle. "And do your pot-smoking mother and current wife and two teenage sons know that you are positive?"

"Yes, the boys are proud of their daddy." He sat up a bit taller. "They see me as a Magic Johnson type."

"Do you live with your sons, mother, and Tawanda?"

"No, they all live in my mother's house. I live with my ex-lover."

I looked at my obnoxious stick figure and then realized why so many people drew them. I attached a noose around its neck and broke the crayon in two.

Butler appeared with the wine and I drank half of it down.

DeWitt's cell rang again, and I jumped at the opportunity to escape to the men's room.

"Kent, is that property still for sale?"

Once in there, I splashed water on my face and looked hard at myself in the mirror. My head was swirling from the wine; my thoughts were spinning from too much information. *Curtis, you have a choice here. You can leave. You don't have to stay.*

I came out of the bathroom chanting to myself, *I'm going to leave, I'm going to leave.* I sat back down next to DeWitt.

He was just finishing the phone call. "We'll come by and see it tomorrow." He hooked his cell onto his belt loop and grabbed my hand.

DeWitt explained to me that there was a beautiful parcel of land for sale just outside Bridgehampton. It was a little peninsula, an oasis, just waiting for the two of us to build our dream home on it.

This guy was too much. "I think I'm busy tomorrow."

"Change your plans."

I just laughed and reached for the red wine. DeWitt slipped a ring off the third finger of his left hand and presented it to me.

"Will you marry me, babe?"

I looked him straight in the eye. "Yes. Oops, sorry, you're already married. I don't think so."

He held the ring out to me. "I'm giving it to you."

"But I don't want it, DeWitt."

Butler arrived with the calamari. It looked like it was squirming as much as I was.

Suddenly that charming cell phone went off again. *Please answer it, DeWitt.* He answered it as I pushed my plate away and dipped the focaccia in the tearstained olive oil.

"Stryker, I can't lend you any more money. The rent's overdue, and you owe for last month, too. Man, I can't talk now. I'm on a date." He closed his phone again and started carving the pale, rubbery squid on his plate.

"Don't tell me. The ex-lover?"

"A great guy, just not applying himself."

In other words, he's lazy and out of work, and DeWitt is supporting him. I took a peek at my watch as his knife struggled with the slippery squid. "When did you two split up?"

"Three years ago."

I looked to the ceiling.

"Babe. I wouldn't normally tell a first date this, but . . ."

What else could he tell me? What else could he possibly pull out of the hat?

"Stryker was arrested last weekend."

Somehow, I wasn't surprised. I wondered if it was drug-related. Theft-related? Armed robbery-related?

"And I had to bail him out of jail."

Sarcastically, I asked, "Couldn't you have just left him in there?" I took a well-needed hit of merlot.

"His sister didn't like it when I did that to him the last time."

"The last time? He's been arrested before? What was the charge?"

"Stryker has a fetish. He was arrested for trespassing and indecent exposure."

I'm amazed. He got me on this one. I would never have guessed. This actually piqued my interest. "He was trespassing where and exposing to whom?"

"He's an exhibitionist." DeWitt's eyes opened wide and I swear his nostrils flared. "Do you thrive on nude beaches?"

I choked on my wine. "No, I do not."

He told me that Stryker had tasteful pictures of himself nude in front of great tourist places like the Empire State Building, Saint Patrick's Cathedral, and the Best Buy on 23rd Street.

I knew the wine was starting to hit me because I didn't question the Best Buy. "But . . . what if there are children around?"

DeWitt looked both ways to make sure no one was listening. "Stryker is very sensitive to that. He'll make sure the coast is clear."

When I asked where he was when he was arrested this time, he said that Stryker's latest kick was to enter a section of state property along the Long Island Expressway. In the woods, he would take all of his clothes off and then run out and along the highway so motorists could see him totally naked. Then he would dart back into the woods.

"Is he attractive?"

DeWitt sadly shook his head.

"Pity. But that's so dangerous."

"A couple of times, cars have nearly hit him."

I thought it was dangerous for the drivers. Imagine this nude creature coming out of the woods and running alongside them. They probably thought he was a shaved deer or something.

DeWitt said he had to take a cash advance on his credit card to bail Stryker out of jail and confessed that he was a bit short on money.

"Can you pick up this tab, babe?"

"You know what, DeWitt? I'm going to pick up something." I squiggled my way out from the banquette. "I'm going to pick up my tired ass and frazzled brain, and I'm going to leave. You ordered it, you pay for it."

"But babe," he cried, reaching out for my hands. I managed to pull them away. "It's you and me now."

"But *babe*, it's not." And at top volume and full projection, I said, "You know that line of yours, 'I'm a beacon of light'? 'Gay men are attracted to me like moths to a flame'? It may be true. But what you don't warn them of is that if they get too close to the flame, they get burned! Well, this little moth escaped."

And with that, I proudly made an extraordinary exit, bowing to my attentive audience.

≥ ≤

One week later and I was still thinking about that parcel of land DeWitt spoke of that was located in Bridgehampton. So I did some research and found out on the Web that it did exist and that it was still available.

I rented a car, drove out to see it, and, true enough, it was absolutely breathtaking. It really was an oasis. I knew even before seeing it that it was much too expensive for me to afford. Still, I just had to take a look at it and dream.

But as I was driving home on the Long Island Expressway, right about North Babylon, traffic came to a dead stop. Fearing a horrific accident had occurred, I looked out of the passenger-side window as two state troopers were arresting a nude man on the side of the highway.

I couldn't believe it. Stryker must be streaking again. But as I looked closer, I realized it was DeWitt.

THIRTEEN

COMEUPPANCE

After the disastrous dates with Park and DeWitt, I felt I had to pull out all the stops and try to meet someone of substance and quality. I was nervous about sharing these two encounters with Dr. Tunick. Did I think she would judge me? No. Did I want to save face? Yes, and meet a terrific guy.

So, after doing extensive research in bookstores and on the Internet and asking trusted friends and colleagues where and how I could find my partner, on the recommendation of a total stranger on the subway, I became a member of Quality Queers, a dating service.

For a onetime lifetime-membership fee, this company promised to match you with the love of your life. They took pictures and then had me fill out a questionnaire. They do the matching. Their concept is that if you do it, you're more than likely to pick a loser, the way you have in the past. Nice initial positive reinforcement. Once they review your likes and dislikes, they play matchmaker and then send you a picture and a profile of your mate. And I had just received mine over the Internet.

Unable not to share everything with Quinn, I leapt for the telephone. He was in his car on the 10, heading west toward Santa Monica in the middle of a torrential downpour. Although every mountainside was lush and beautiful with flowers and greenery, the rainy season should have been over by now.

"Los Angeles is sliding away," he exclaimed. "I now have

what I always wanted."

There was so much static on the line. "What's that?"

"A pool in my backyard." He laughed. "It was my neighbors', who live farther up the canyon."

I couldn't hold back my excitement any longer. "I got the picture of my mate."

Quinn was in bumper-to-bumper traffic, slow as molasses. "How much did this cost you?"

I hesitated sharing and wondered if I should lie, but I didn't. "Five thousand dollars."

He screamed, "Shit, for five thousand dollars, I'll date you!"

Somehow, this wasn't the support I had been looking for. He wanted more details, but first I wanted to remind him of a man we had seen several years earlier.

On a late-summer Friday evening, while Quinn and I were walking in front of the Metropolitan Museum of Art, God's gift to men, women, and children jogged by us.

He was a stallion whose pectoral muscles bounced so manfully and erotically with every stride he took toward us. Unfortunately, he kept running—past us. And he had not only the body of a God but the face to go with it, too.

Quinn reminded me, "He looked just like a straight Ricky Martin." And then he started to cry, and by cry I mean sob.

"Yes, Quinn, I'm sure that man's beauty has caused many people to cry."

"No," he whined. "The 405 just kicked in, and we have come to a complete stop on the freeway." He blew his nose. "This is maddening. Distract me."

I told him that my match was flawless. He had a more massive chest than the stallion and a more beautiful face than Ricky's. As I skimmed through his profile, I noticed he did something that had to do with law.

"Quinn, I think he's a paralegal, and we have a gazillion

things in common, and he lives in TriBeCa, and isn't all of this too cool?" I gushed at him.

"Yes, Gidget," Quinn laughed. "What's his name?"

I took my time and said it very dramatically. "Eric Cornell."

"Curtis Cornell, I like the sound of that."

Then it dawned on me. "Quinn, I've never been with an Eric. Maybe it's an omen?"

"Maybe you need to move to another city, 'cuz after Eric, you've dated everyone else in New York."

Eric and I had spoken briefly on the phone earlier that day, and he was going to call back to make dinner plans. Just then, my other line beeped in.

I looked at my caller id. "Oh my God, it's him." I started to hyperventilate. "Quinn, how's my voice?"

"Rough, thin, scratchy?"

I relaxed, took another breath and purred, "Hello?"

Quinn paused. "You sound like a female Eartha Kitt."

I tried again in a higher register. "Hello?"

"Too Miss America." Quinn giggled. "Once more, with feeling."

Flustered, I switched lines and murmured, "Asshole."

"I didn't know you cared." Eric laughed.

"Eric?" I took a breath and lowered my voice. "Hello."

"I like asshole better," he said, laughing harder. "Is that how you always answer the phone, Curtis?"

I told him it was a long story and that I was on the line with my best friend of twenty-four years.

"Bet the two of you have a lot of history there."

I laughed, thinking, *I could write a book.*

"Well, I'm impressed," Eric continued. "Friendships that old are rare and important."

"Yeah, Quinn is old...but medium rare." We both laughed and suddenly I realized I was being myself.

"Curtis, do you mind coming down to my neighborhood for dinner?"

"I'd love to."

"How about Nono?"

Nono was a gourmet Japanese restaurant that was harder to get into than a wet pair of leather pants. As with many neighborhoods in New York City and like my mother, names are often nicked. *TriBeCa* means triangle below Canal Street. *Soho* means South of Houston Street. *Noho* means North of Houston Street. And Nono means . . . North of North? What *does* that mean?

Eric added, "It's kind of my hangout."

You're kind of my guy, I thought. Then I caught myself. *Pull back the reins, Curtis, and go slow.*

"I'd love to go to Nono."

"Good," he said. "See you at nine thirty?"

⋛ ⋜

Unfortunately, I went too slowly. The first setback was the nose strip. I've never been prone to pimples, but blackheads I do suffer from. While trying on every piece of clothing I own, I left the damn thing on too long and then ripped it off too fast, taking most of my nose with it. And to top that off, I was forced to take a bus all the way down to Hudson and Franklin streets from the Upper West Side.

So, with the tip of my nose bleeding and my armpits dripping (and I'm the one who doesn't sweat), I made my graceful entrance into Nono almost a half-hour late.

Searching for my mate at the bar, the hostess approached me.

"Can I help you, sir?"

For a split second I panicked. Did he leave? Was I stood up? "I was supposed to meet—"

"Are you Curtis?" she asked, smiling.

"Yes, I am," I said, surprised.

"Mr. Cornell is waiting for you at his table. Please, follow me."

And with that I was escorted past the high-fashion models, actors whose names I never remember, and the financial investors who make much too much money. We weren't seated in the middle of the room where everyone could obviously see you, but at a much more discreet and private table in the back. And there I met Mr. Eric Cornell, God's gift to men, women, children, and more men.

"Please don't get up," I said.

He let out a laugh. "I like your sense of humor, Curtis."

"Did I say something funny?"

"And your modesty."

Stunned at Eric's physical beauty, I nervously started chattering away. "I'm sorry I'm so late. Really, I'm sorry. Usually I'm right on time or even early, and I'm embarrassed to say that I've never been here before. Everyone talks about Nono and the food and the atmosphere and the celebrities and how hard it is to get in, and I just figured by the time I got down here and into this place it probably would be passé, or maybe closed, or—"

"Hi," he whispered, gently interrupting me.

I took a deep breath, "Hi."

"You're even more attractive than your picture."

"Thank you," I said quietly. "So are you."

Absorbing the moment, we sat there for I don't know how long, just looking at each other.

The waiter broke our trance. "Can I get you something from the bar?"

"Ketel One martini straight up with a twist, please," Eric ordered.

"And I'll have a Maker's Mark manhattan straight up with a cherry."

"Very good," said the waiter.

I came out with, "Our drinks are going to look great together."

Eric burst into laughter. "I *really* love your sense of humor."

But I meant it. "You with your crystal clear martini, me with my deep mahogany manhattan. We'll be the envy of drinkers all over the city."

He thought for a moment. "Not to mention the glasses they come in are so classy."

"And great props, too," I added. "And the beautiful thing is that our drinks are similar but different. Eric, you have a twist."

"Curtis, you have a cherry." He winked.

"Your martini is cool, suave, and sophisticated."

"And your manhattan is warm, heady, and luxurious." Another long beat as we just smiled at each other.

I gasped. "I need a drink."

"And here we are, gentlemen," said the waiter as he slowly set our very large, filled-to-the-brims libations down onto the table.

We gingerly picked up our glasses.

Eric toasted. "Here's to complementary opposites."

≳ ≲

The food was sublime, I think. Actually, I paid very little attention to it.

"Eric, do you like to travel?"

"I don't do it as often as I'd like, but yes."

I told him that I felt as though I was born with one foot in the middle of the road. But the odd thing was that I thought I enjoyed planning the trips even more than taking them, that I loved the researching of a new, maybe exotic, place I've never been to before.

"Where have you been?" Eric asked, seeming truly interested and eager to hear what I had to say.

"Madrid, Florence, Venice, London, Edinburgh, Amsterdam."

"Paris?"

"Not yet." I blushed a little. "I know this is going to sound silly, but I've been putting off Paris. I travel alone most of the time. And even though I have friends in Paris who keep begging me to come, I want to go when—"

"You're in love?" he asked, smiling.

"Am I that much of a cliché?"

"No, you're that much of a romantic."

"I just don't want to be looking at some magnificent church or breathtaking view or charming shop, and turn and say, 'Oh my God, this is so beautiful,' and not have anyone there to share it with who is important and special to me."

"I understand. I've been putting Paris off, too."

"Gentlemen," the waiter said while putting the check on the table. "Sorry, but the restaurant is closing."

We both looked at our watches and simultaneously said, "Time flies . . ."

"What's the damage?" I asked, trying to reach for the check.

"My treat, Curtis."

"No, let me—"

"You can get the next one. That is, if you'll have dinner with me again?"

"Thank you, and I'd love to." It's then that I looked around the restaurant and noticed that it was totally empty of patrons. "I can't remember the last time I closed a restaurant."

"Your stimulating and enjoyable company sent me into a time warp," Eric said.

"Thank you. But it didn't help that I was late. I was going to take the subway, but there was no downtown service due to a water-main break, and then—up aboveground—there wasn't a cab in sight, so, like I said, I ended up taking a bus down here. You know, one of those new accordion ones that hold too many people and take too long for everyone to get on and get off, and then at some point a woman in a wheelchair had to get on the bus, and that takes forever, not that they don't deserve to ride public transportation like the rest of us, but it can be so frustrating sometimes when you're rushing to get somewhere important and you're just waiting for the whole ordeal to be over with and so, I'm sorry that I was late."

"No, problem," Eric reassured me as he twisted around and pulled his jacket off of the back of his chair. "I have to make a quick trip to the men's room."

And with that, Eric didn't get up out of his chair but instead rolled it away from the table. He was in a wheelchair. I was panic-stricken. *How could I have missed this?* Noticing the fear registering on my face and the lack of words emanating from my mouth, Eric pushed himself next to me.

"You didn't know?"

"I'm so . . . so embarrassed."

"It should have been in my profile."

"I read it kind of quickly. I noticed how much we had in common and that you are a para— Oh my God." I felt my face turn beet-red.

"It's okay," Eric assured. "You still want to have another dinner?"

"Of course. Of course I do," I said with shameful doubt.

"Good, because I want to, too. Complementary opposites, remember?"

Eric gently touched my arm, which sent shivers through my entire body, and then exited to the men's room. I am such a jerk. When he returned, I stood up and wasn't sure if I should walk ahead of him or stay behind and push. He intuitively saved the moment.

"Go ahead, Curtis. This is how I get in my arm workouts."

I agreed. "And they're sure paying off."

Relieved that he seemed okay with my major faux pas, I felt some of the embarrassment drain from my face.

≩ ≦

Later that night, I strolled as Eric rolled alongside the Hudson River.

"I take it you've never dated a paraplegic before?"

"It shows?" I asked nervously. "I mean, I've never met one before. I mean . . . I mean—"

"I think you mean well."

"I do, Eric. I'm just trying to see if I can stick both of my feet into my mouth at the same time." Thank goodness he smiled. "It's just that this situation has never presented itself before."

"I understand."

We strolled and rolled in silence.

"So, if you're not a paralegal, what do you do?" I sheepishly asked.

He shared with me that he was an attorney. Litigation was his specialty. He went to Princeton and then Columbia and found that school was exciting, challenging, and hopeful.

In the early years, Eric paid his dues, bouncing from one small office to the next, realizing very quickly that what the bosses wanted were quick settlements. Orders were: Do anything, but don't end up in the courtroom.

He was disappointed and disenchanted, because that was the part that he liked. But Eric hung in there and now, at age forty-seven, he had his own firm and was proud to say that they weren't just about billing. His office really did care about its clients, their lives, and their rights.

Eric misread my face. "I'm boring you, aren't I?"

Actually, I was mesmerized. "No, quite the contrary. A lawyer with integrity."

"And you're a writer?"

"Yes, but a late bloomer." I told him about growing up in Westchester and then going to the University of Massachusetts, initially majoring in pre-veterinary medicine.

"I love animals," I declared.

"So do I." We smiled at each other.

"I inherited an innate understanding of science and math from my dad, who passed a while back."

Eric asked, "What did he do?"

I was about to give one of my stock answers when for the first time I decided to tell the truth. "My dad was a good but simple chemist."

"That's a decent profession," Eric said. I agreed, feeling good about what had just happened. "But, ultimately, I didn't have it in me to be a veterinarian."

"What do you mean?"

I explained to him that in an attempt to weed out the faint of heart, the veterinary school has you deal with barnyard creatures first. We had to artificially inseminate chickens.

"How the hell do you do that?" he asked.

"You grab a cock, turn it upside down, stroke it until it gets excited, and then you catch the semen in a cup."

There was silence, and then Eric burst into laughter. "So, what else is new?"

I swore it was the truth. He could ask anyone who has gone through pre-vet. But stroking cocks didn't turn me off, equestrian rectal examinations did.

Case in point: I was second in line to perform my first exam. The female student in front of me slipped on her pre-lubed, Holly Golightly, up-to-the-shoulder plastic opera gloves and approached her unsuspecting victim—cautiously, of course. Normally, they told us, rear entry was no problem for the examiner or the horse. But with a wrong twist here and probably a long fingernail there, the mare bucked and broke the poor girl's arm in three different places.

"Damn!" exclaimed Eric.

"I threw up and changed my major to theater."

"Did you pursue acting?"

"In New York. And I'm proud to say I made a living at it. I had to, because I couldn't keep a job as a waiter."

Eric laughed.

"I did lots of bus-and-trucks and dinner theater but after five years of wondering where the next job was going to come from or feeling like I was only as good as my last show, I decided to go into a safe, secure, steady profession like writing."

"Very stable," Eric added with a smile.

"First children's books, then plays, and, when I'm lucky, a screenplay here and there."

I felt I had talked too much, said too much. We stopped in silence and looked out at the river. I sat down on a park bench, and he wheeled over to me. Sensing my self-consciousness, Eric slipped his arm through mine. For me, the Hudson never looks magical, but tonight, with a tugboat passing by and the Jersey lights twinkling beyond, I felt like we were in Paris.

"Would you like to go on another date, Curtis?"

"Yes, I would," I said too quickly.

"Are you eager or just nervous?"

I honestly said, "A little of both."

"We've talked about everything but the wheelchair," Eric said with a smile.

I felt as though I had made a big mistake. "I'm sorry. I didn't know if I should bring it up."

"I should be making this easier for you."

I grabbed his huge biceps. "It's not hard at all, believe me."

"Well, that's disappointing."

I didn't get the double entendre at first but then smiled. There was an awkward pause.

"Yes, I have sensations from the waist down," he said softy.

"Can you . . . ?"

"Yes, I can get an erection."

The moon's glow reflected off the river and onto Eric's face. I leaned over and held my head next to his. The warmth of his body dispelled the chill in the air. I pulled away slightly, and we looked at each other. Eyes wide open, our lips touched, and we kissed.

≥ ≤

Two seconds hadn't passed since I left Eric that night and I was back on the phone with Quinn.

"You're *still* stuck in traffic?" I put the phone down and covered the mouthpiece as I laughed out loud.

"Can you fucking believe this?" Quinn grabbed his steering wheel and strangled it till his knuckles turned white. "I'm stuck in front of the Hollywood Bowl. There must have been an accident."

I tried to calm him down with male distraction. "Any cute guys stuck with you?"

He cried, "No one will look at me. Not when I'm driving my boat."

Quinn was right. This successful Hollywood writer took to riding the streets of Los Angeles in a 1980 Buick Century Limited four-dour luxury sedan. The funny part is that they had the nerve to call it a "luxury." It was hideous, and large enough to house a homeless refugee family of thirteen. Why he wouldn't spend the money on a new car was a mystery to me. A man magnet this vehicle wasn't.

Quinn wanted more details about Eric. "So, after dinner and the stroll along the river?"

"We kissed," I stopped to catch my breath. "My God, Quinn, can this man kiss."

"And sex?" he asked impishly.

I nonchalantly threw it away. "Not yet."

Quinn tapped the phone with his finger. "Excuse me?"

"You told me not to rush it."

He laughed. "Since when did you ever listen to me, Curtis? What's up? There's something you're not telling me."

"Well, just one little thing."

Quinn was beside himself. "Yes, yes?"

"Eric is—" I took a deep breath—"a paraplegic."

He corrected me. "You mean a paralegal."

"I thought he was, but I found out he's a paraplegic."

"Oh my God, Curtis, is he in a wheelchair?"

I just about lost it. "No Quinn, he just drags himself along the street."

Quinn was silent for a moment and then asked the question: "Can he get an erection?"

I reprimanded him. "Quinn, that question is just so . . . pedestrian. Of course he can get an erection."

He wouldn't let up. "How do you know?"

"Because he told me so. And I told him I was poz."

The traffic Quinn was sitting in started to move slowly. "And?"

"He's negative but totally fine with it. In fact, he said he's more comfortable being with someone positive 'cause we will definitely be having safe sex. He said negative guys with negative guys tend to be more risky."

"He's got a point there."

"We're going bowling."

"Bowling?" Like nothing had happened, traffic picked up to normal speed. Quinn was looking out his windows, left, right, front, and back.

"Yes, and I don't mean candlepin. I'm talking duckpin."

"Yes, dear. I know you like the big balls."

"Gotta run, Quinn."

"Where's the goddamned fucking car accident? What was

clogging everything up? This infuriates me."

I'm sure he continued ranting and raving for twenty minutes after I hung up.

≷ ≶

After twenty-five years of living in New York City and nagging all of my friends and selective dates to go bowling with me, I find it ironic that the person I finally threw gutter balls with—and he's the one who suggested the activity, mind you—was in a wheelchair.

Eric told me to meet him at the Port Authority Bus Station. My first thought was, *Yikes, too dangerous.* Whenever a friend or relative has come into the city via the bus terminal, embarrassing as that is, I've cleverly asked them to meet me a block south or north or east or even west. That place is more frightening than slipping through the metal detector at Bell's nightclub down on 14th Street. But then I remembered the coast is clear. All those thugs have left Port Authority and are now skulking up and down Christopher Street between 7th Avenue and the West Side Highway.

Relieved yet still holding on to my wallet, I entered the terminal and headed to the second floor on the west side and opened the doors to Leisure Time Bowl. It was beautiful. Leave it to me to discover this fashionable and lively place years after celebrities and athletes made it cool and popular. I'm so hip.

"Hey, Curtis!" hollered Eric as he sped over to me. "I've got us a lane."

"Eric, do we still rent your shoes, like in the old days?"

"You do, I don't," he said.

I should think before I speak. "I bet you have your own ball, don't you?"

He pulled out a Day-Glo green one.

"Good, then I'm grabbing a shocking pink one."

The glory of electronic scoring monitors took my attention away from the thought that after this fabulous night out on the town, I would suffer for the rest of my life with plantar warts passed on to me by some early inhabitant of my truly deformed rental bowling shoes.

But then there was Eric. I could watch him for hours. He would unself-consciously wheel his chair up to his mark and, like anyone standing on two feet, he'd bring the ball up to his nose and target his sight. He'd then lean to his right, and I drooled each time the veins in his arms bulged under the weight of his ball.

Like a perfect pendulum, he would arc back and at the height of the backswing, there was a split second when everything stopped and his triceps would contract and then suddenly Eric would let it all go, allowing his arm to swing forward, and the ball would explode out of his hand. Damn, I had no idea bowling was so erotic.

"Strike!" I screamed. "You're a great bowler, Eric."

"You're not too bad yourself, considering you haven't played in umpteen years."

I stood in front of him, grabbed the arms of his chair, and leaned in to his face and whispered, "And I can ride a unicycle, too."

"Can I see?"

I spun away. "It'll cost you."

"What?" he asked, laughing.

"As a kid, I used to charge neighbors to watch me. But I'll let you watch for free." I sauntered over to my bowling ball.

"I like the sound of that."

I grabbed my pink ball, dried my hand professionally on the side of my pants, took my mark, bent slightly forward, and set my sights. I took one step as I let the ball swing down, second step for the backswing, and just as I took my third step for the release, Eric yelled out, "Nice butt!"

Startled, I twisted to look back at him and let go of the ball. It flew into the lane next to us and guttered down the alley.

"No fair," I shouted. "You distracted me."

He laughed. "You didn't know bowling was so cutthroat?"

"I didn't know it was so sexual."

I took my mark for my second throw. Looking back at him very seductively, I said, "No comments from the peanut gallery." He just smiled. I set my sights. One step, two step, and as I was taking the third, he shouted, "Hot wiggle!"

Laughing so hard, I released the ball and it left my hand with so little force that it plopped down on the lane and slowly—oh so slowly—inched its way toward the pins, finally, pathetically knocking one over.

"And it's a hit," Eric shouted.

"What you're doing is illegal. I could sue you, Mr. Lawyer, for sexually harassing the bowler."

"Come on, Pinky." He laughed. "You're on a roll."

I warned him, "It's all fun and games till someone loses an eye."

And the way I was handling that ball, someone would. This time I really focused. I may have a great sense of humor, but I'm also fiercely competitive. *Concentrate, Curtis.* I felt performance anxiety. I wiped my hand. One step, two, step, three step . . . release.

My ball traveled down the lane at breakneck speed and . . . whammo!

"Strike!" Eric yelled.

I squatted down, jumped up with all my might, and did a half-twist to Eric, screaming, "Yes!" and promptly came down on the side of my ankle.

I hollered out in pain.

Eric wheeled over, calling out, "You okay?"

I sat down on the lane, rubbing my ankle as Eric patted my head.

"Just a twist." I winced as I rotated my foot.

"Enough bowling for one night."

"Guess it's better than losing an eye." I stood up and put weight on the foot. It was sore but manageable.

As I started to walk, Eric came up beside me and said, "No way. That injury is much too severe for you to walk on."

"What are you talking about? It's fine," I reassured him.

"Nope, hop on board," he said, patting his thighs. "Sit on my lap."

At first I hesitated, looking around, and then I saw his beaming face, his incredible smile. And then I dramatically feigned a severely injured leg.

"Oh, thank you, kind sir. I seem to have hurt my ankle and I can't walk. Can you help me? Can you take care of me?" I gently sat down on his lap.

He did an excellent Groucho Marx impersonation. "Can I ever? But first, a complete examination is required."

We sped away with my arms around his neck. He zoomed out of the alley, down the elevator, and through the parking garage to a red sport-utility van.

Eric beeped open the sliding door, and a lift automatically descended. We rolled on board and he locked his chair into where the driver's seat would be. I hopped off of his lap and buckled in to the passenger's side.

"This is so incredible," I gasped.

"See here? The gas and breaks I work with hand controls. Kinda like a motorcycle."

"Eric, this is too cool."

And with that he drove me home to his loft in TriBeCa.

≥ ≤

·)≥   ≤(·

"Your place could be in *Architectural Digest*," I whispered as we entered.

"It has," he whispered back. "I designed it myself."

And he had scaled everything so he could reach it from his chair.

He asked me if I was hungry, but honestly, the last thing on my mind was food, so I shrugged it off.

He teased me with, "I have some lobster salad and chilled champagne."

"I'm starving."

He laughed. "See, I did read your profile."

This man was too much. And after two helpings of lobster he asked, "Would you like some more?"

Was he insane? I could never get enough of it. So I asked in my best Oliver voice, "Please, sir, I want some more And Veuve Clicquot. A man after my own heart."

"I am," he said quietly.

Suddenly, I was very nervous, so I shifted the conversation away from myself and asked him to tell me more about his upbringing.

He grew up in Pittsburgh, and his dad passed about five years ago. Tragically, his mother died when he was just eleven. He had no siblings and just a few aunts and uncles that he had lost touch with.

He said in a confessional tone, "It's probably funny to hear a grown man say this, but when Dad died, all of a sudden I felt like an orphan."

There was silence, and I wondered if this was the time to ask him about his paralysis. Was he born with it, or did a disease or an accident bring it on? The timing just didn't seem right.

With candles burning low, Eric signaled to me to head to the living room.

As we crossed the loft, the lights in the dining room and kitchen went out and the ones in the living room dimmed.

"How did that happen?"

"Magic." Eric laughed. "Actually, I have a remote in my hand." He handed it to me as I sat down on the sofa. He had rigged the whole system himself. The remote not only controlled the lights but also an automatic lock on the door.

"I can even turn the oven on from the bedroom."

"I bet you can," I said with a wicked smile. And then I looked over at him sitting before me. "Eric, you constantly amaze me. Is there anything you *can't* do?"

After a pensive moment, he said, "Walk?" There was silence. "Can I ask for your help onto the couch?"

"Of course," I said, jumping to my feet. Zealously and without thinking, I reached out for his hands and pulled him toward me, and in one swift move we both ended up on the rug. He started to laugh first and then I followed.

"I'm sorry," I finally said, once I caught my breath.

"For what? That's the best laugh I've had in years."

I came to a sitting position. "I guess I should have picked you up?"

"What were you thinking?" Eric asked, still laughing.

"I wasn't. See the affect you have on me?"

"Have you seen the affect you have on me?" Eric asked as he pulled himself closer to me. I laid back and he slipped his forearm behind my head, like a pillow. The safety I felt within his arms allowed me to totally surrender.

Examining my face, he stroked my eyebrow, brushed my cheek, and gently nuzzled my earlobe with his nose. "I dream of the day when I can lie with my head in your lap while you read to me anything and everything you've ever written."

Gazing into his eyes, I recited, "His beauty shall in these black lines be seen, and they shall live, and he in them, still green."

"Did you write that?"

"No, Shakespeare."

"Well, it's still beautiful." He smiled.

Time stood still as his mouth descended on mine, and he kissed me so deeply and so passionately for so long that it truly felt as though it were the first time I had ever been kissed in my life.

"I have but only kissed you, Curtis," he whispered.

And without another word spoken, I lifted Eric up into my arms and carried him into his bedroom.

≳ ≲

Quinn ran down Santa Monica Boulevard in West Hollywood after parking his car in a garage as I headed uptown on Broadway in a cab.

"Curtis," he said breathlessly, "I can only talk a second. I'm late for my back waxing."

"Didn't you stop that due to a staph infection?"

"Those were my balls."

I grimaced. "Honestly, you gays."

"Speaking of which, how's Eric?"

My cabbie veered sharply to the left, avoiding a car pulling out from nowhere, causing me to fall onto my side. "I think I'm falling hard and fast."

"Curtis, hard and fast for you is on the first date. You've been seeing each other for almost two weeks. This is a long-term relationship."

"Very funny. So, how is the Colt?"

"I have to break up with him."

My cab came to an abrupt stop at a red light, and I nearly hit my head on the divider.

"Curtis, my pony only wants to ride bareback."

"And how do you feel about that?"

There was a long pause. "I'd love to be having sex wearing nothing, but I'm just not comfortable taking the risk. And there's other stuff. I just don't know how to end it."

"You say something vague like, 'We aren't a match.' You don't owe him any explanation. It's not like you've declared you are lovers, right?"

"Right, but—"

"All's fair in love and war."

My light turned green and the cabbie floored it, causing my head to whip back.

"I guess so. What are you and Eric doing tonight?"

"Dinner on the Upper East Side. His work schedule has been crazy, and he's had to cancel several of our most recent dates. He said there's something important he wants to talk about. I think I'm going to say the L-word."

"Lesbian?"

I let out a hysterical scream, and the cabbie jammed on the breaks. I must've scared him, because he turned around and started yelling at me in what sounded like Arabic. I gave him an apologetic smile.

"Curtis, do I hear wedding bells in Vermont?"

That reminded me that I should ask Eric whether he's been to New England. And I should ask him if he's ever skied. But more important, I should ask how he became paralyzed. I should— I stopped my thought mid-sentence, hearing myself using the word *should*. *Should* just oozed with guilt. We *should* eliminate *should* from the dictionary.

The cab driver was really angry and didn't seem to want to take me any further. I tried to ignore him.

"Quinn, what am I doing? I've met the man of my dreams and he's confined to a wheelchair." I motioned to the driver to go on, but he just kept screaming. "And I'm walking on eggshells, fearful that at any moment something politically incorrect is going to come flying out of my mouth and . . . "

My cabbie wasn't going to budge, so I hunted for money as other cars started honking at us. Why couldn't he have pulled over instead of stopping right in the middle of Broadway?

"Curtis, you are the most PC person I know."

I looked at the meter and threw the driver just enough money to cover it. "Goddamn foreigner," I mumbled as I jumped out.

"Quinn, what's developing between Eric and me is just so wonderful and new and different that I have moments of sheer panic." A car zoomed by, just barely missing me.

"Do you want me to send you some Ativan?"

"There isn't a pill big enough," I declared as I started walking uptown.

"Relax and be your charming self. Everybody loves you."

We hung up and I stood on the corner of 72nd Street, looking at my watch, waiting for the light to change, when out of nowhere a cab came barreling toward me. People on the sidewalk jumped back as the car screeched to a halt so close to me that it brushed the front of my pants.

Stunned, like a gay caught in Middle Eastern headlights, I stood there as the cabbie opened the window, threw my money back into my face, and then sped off, shouting some unintelligible curse. *Everybody loves me.*

≳ ≲

From the get-go, I knew my sessions with Dr. Tunick were out of the ordinary, but now I was beginning to wonder. Granted, she was recommended to me by Quinn, which would make anyone question everything, but during this session I was basically helping her prepare her apartment to be painted.

Any doubts I had about her professionalism were immediately erased by the fact that I knew she was helping me.

"Dr. Tunick, my mother is a lesbian with boundaries," I

declared, reaching as high as I could to take down a portrait of some ancient relative of hers from over the fireplace.

"And that makes you feel?"

"I don't know. I'm still trying to digest it. It's hard." The stepladder I was standing on wobbled, causing one of my feet to slide off a rung. I scraped my shin and just counted the seconds before the stinging would begin. Dr. Tunick had her back to me and hadn't noticed. What I continued with was more painful than my shin. "It's hard enough for me to picture my mother having sex with a man, never mind a woman."

She took the portrait from me. "Why picture her having sex with anyone at all?" she asked, smiling.

She had a point there. "It's hard not to do when she's a walking PDA."

"PDA?"

"Public display of affection." She leaned the picture against the far wall and moved the ladder to one of the two side windows. I was upset that I hadn't noticed these windows before. Granted, they were virtually impossible to see in the dark room, but I fancied myself someone very observant.

"You do have to remember that she is not just your mother. She's also a woman with womanly needs."

"And she told Quinn before me. She told him ages ago." Dr. Tunick gave me the end of an old sheet, and together we threw it over furniture that we had pushed into the center of the room.

"And who did you tell first when you found out you were HIV-positive? You didn't tell your mother for fear of her reaction. Maybe she feels the same way about you?"

"Dr. Tunick, I feel so raw. Like my heart is on my sleeve."

Together we put a sheet over the organ.

"You're feeling alive. Just remember that you can't dictate the way that people act or react. But you do have control over your own reactions to things. And Curtis, strive to be honest,

honest with yourself."

"You should go on *Oprah*."

She laughed. "I don't know about that, but I am going to Poland."

I felt a flash of panic. *She's leaving me?*

"When?" I asked in a desperate tone.

"Two weeks from yesterday. It's my older sister's birthday."

She has an older sibling?

"And I found a great round-trip airfare on the Internet. I scheduled the apartment to be painted while I was gone. So we'll just skip our next session and I'll see you in a month."

Like an abandoned child, I searched for reasons for her not to go. "But what about Emily-Mae?"

She laughed again. "Mrs. French, on the second landing, is going to take her in."

She picked the dog up from her chair, set her on the floor, and started to walk me to the door.

"Wait, I forgot to tell you all about this really nice guy I met. I think he might be the one."

"Hold on to it, Curtis. It's fresh. It's new. And it's yours. Talking about him now will only diminish what you have."

"But it's going so well."

She smiled. "Then you can tell me all about him when I get back."

She slid her parlor door open as Emily-Mae chewed on my pant leg. Suddenly, my eyes were blinded by a flash of sunlight reflecting off a stainless-steel table situated in the front of the room. Dr. Tunick had taken the heavy curtains down, and I realized that it was the table that I had stubbed my toe on weeks earlier.

"Dr. Tunick, I like it with the dark drapes gone. They don't suit you."

"I agree. I'm going to take the ones down in my bedroom, too. After the apartment is painted, I think I'll put up some sheers. It's time for a change. Thank you, Curtis, for helping me with this."

"No problem. Have a safe trip, Dr. Tunick."

I so wanted to embrace her but felt maybe that was inappropriate. Instead, I awkwardly stretched out my hand and she shook it graciously.

She bent down and pulled Emily-Mae off my pant leg and pushed her into the apartment. "Good-bye, Curtis." She smiled and slid the massive door shut.

≥ ≤

Later that night, I unself-consciously walked with my hand on Eric's shoulder down East 82nd Street, heading toward his van, which was parked near the Metropolitan Museum of Art.

We had just had dinner at a French bistro, Le Boeuf Neuf. The food was superb and the atmosphere very romantic. However, just as we were leaving, there was an incident with his chair. An elderly woman was trying to pass by him and caught her foot on the wheel. She fell and hurt herself pretty badly. When the EMS crew whisked her away, they confirmed that she had broken her leg.

I found the whole ordeal morbidly amusing; however, I was smart enough to keep that to myself. And I assumed that Eric's silence once we got out onto the street was due to the fact that he was thinking about the pending lawsuit.

But he had seemed distant and distracted even before the accident. Actually, from the moment we met earlier that night.

I started to massage his shoulder as we approached Fifth Avenue, and broke the silence with, "It's quite a coincidence that we both love that restaurant."

"It's one of the few French provincial restaurants that I can get into."

"Eric, you're the man." I said, really butch-like, while punching his arm. "You can get into any place at a moment's notice."

"No, Curtis," he said with quite an angry tone. "I mean there are many restaurants that I love that are not wheelchair-accessible."

"I'm sorry, I wasn't thinking."

He stopped and looked up at me. "You weren't thinking about my chair."

"Honestly, I just don't see it anymore." There was silence as he wheeled ahead of me and turned onto the avenue.

Then he stopped and spun around toward me. "Curtis, saying you don't see my chair is like telling an African-American that you no longer see them as black."

"I didn't mean to offend."

"The chair is now a permanent part of me. You must see it."

We walked on in silence as it started to romantically drizzle. I tried to lighten things up. "Eric, didn't you say there was something important you wanted to talk to me about?" I asked with a mischievous smile.

He stopped and looked at me seriously. "Curtis?"

"Yes?" His pause was a little too long.

"This is really hard for me to say, because I don't want to hurt your feelings, but you and I are not a match."

I just stared at him. I couldn't believe what I thought I had just heard.

Eric continued. "I've really enjoyed getting to know you, but this isn't going to work."

I smiled broadly and started to laugh. "You're joking, right?"

"No, I'm serious."

And he was. It seemed like eons before I could speak again.

"But . . . this is like coming out of nowhere."

"I'm sorry. I've wanted to talk to you about this but just couldn't find the right moment. I sensed you were getting serious about us."

"Well, yes." I shook my head with disbelief. "I thought things were going so great."

"You're a wonderful man. And you're a lot of fun and you have a beautiful body, but—"

"Is it something I said? Or didn't say? Is it because I was ignoring the wheelchair?"

"It's not just the chair. And it's not just because you've never even asked me how I ended up like this—"

I laughed. "That is so ironic, because—"

"Curtis, it's not like we've said we love each other."

I felt like the wind had just been knocked out of me. "No, Eric, we haven't." I took a moment to compose myself. "If that's your decision, I can't force you to . . . " And then I lost it. I needed a reason, any kind of reason. "Is there something you don't like? Or am I not masculine enough? Is my voice too high? Is it my breath?"

Eric laughed, but I was dead serious. "Your breath is sweet and so are you. Don't change a thing."

"I'm just not sweet enough for you," I said sarcastically.

"I'm sorry, Curtis. Really I am."

"Do you still want to be friends?" I couldn't believe I asked that. *Where is my dignity? Where is my pride?*

"I think it's best if we make a clean break of it and go our separate ways."

Suddenly, the romantic drizzle turned into a torrential downpour.

"Okay, if that's the way you feel." Numb, I searched my brain for something, anything, to say.

"Good-bye, Curtis."

And with that, Eric smiled and rolled away from me.

I turned and started running in the opposite direction. It all felt like slow motion at first. I wanted to run away from Eric, run away from life, run away from myself.

How could someone just say, "We're not a match"? What kind of jerk would break up like that, with no clues, no explanation?

I was blinded by rain and tears and running faster than my legs could carry me, and that's when it appeared, out of nowhere, like a phantom ghost. The mammoth creature was taking a sharp right from Fifth Avenue onto 85th Street to traverse Central Park. I tried to stop, but my shoe skidded on the slippery sidewalk.

I hit the bus broadside and was thrown back onto the curb. I was more frightened than hurt, and before I could get back up onto my feet, a man was by my side.

"Are you okay, guy?" he asked with a deep Southern accent.

I thought I had died and gone to heaven because an angel with sandy-colored hair, smoky gray eyes, and the most perfectly shaped lips for kissing was kneeling over me.

"You just ran into that big old accordion bus."

Suddenly, I broke out into laughter. "Karmic lesson."

"And you're so cute." He smiled as he wiped mud off my face with his shirt.

"Where the hell did you come from?" I asked.

"I'm from Paris."

I sat up. "Paris?"

"Paris, Texas, that is."

He helped me to my feet. "Do you want me to call an ambulance or anything?"

"No," I said, brushing off leaves and dirt. "Really, I'm fine."

He gently touched my forehead. "Looks like you're gonna have quite a bump on your head."

It wasn't the first time. "I'll ice it when I get home."

"Do you want me to walk you there?"

"No, really, I'm fine on my own."

"Well, being new in town, I sure could use a friend or two. Can we keep in touch?"

"Sure. My name is Curtis."

"Dell here." He reached into his pocket. "Let me give you my number."

"Dell? As in..."

"Yup, the farmer." He handed me his business card.

I laughed inside and looked at this kind man. I thought to myself, *Grab him, snatch him*. But I was burnt out. I just couldn't do it anymore. I was tired of dreaming and tired of hoping and I was soaking wet with a head that was beginning to swell.

"Give me a call, Curtis. Maybe we can have coffee or something?"

"Sure, Dell, that would be nice." He moved closer to me, and I quickly put out my hand for a formal shake. "Thanks for helping me up."

"My pleasure."

I left Dell, the kind man from Paris, Texas, and as I walked home in the rain, I threw his phone number in the trash.

FOURTEEN

"ANY CHANGE, SIR?"

I was clean for one month. Clean of men and dates and the emotional chaos they were bringing into my life. And to tell you the truth, it felt good. It felt really good. Magda was coming back from Poland the next day, and I couldn't wait to tell her not only how great I felt but also that I had started a new novel.

Quinn was in town for the Daytime Emmy Awards, because his show had been nominated for best writing team. To celebrate, my mother and I were meeting him at the Paradise Hotel for drinks and dinner the night before.

The Paradise was an old, dilapidated midtown hotel that recently went through a delicious renovation. The lobby is sleek and modern, and there's a magnificent floating marble staircase that leads up to the second floor, where the bar and restaurant are located.

I was happy that we were all meeting early in the evening. This would give us a chance to hear one another before the crowds showed up.

I arrived at the bar first, and just as the bartender served me my drink, Quinn made his way up the stairs. He was about to surprise me when all of a sudden he saw what I was putting up to my lips.

"What are you drinking?" he asked horrified.

I spun around and hugged him. "Pinot grigio. I've lost the

taste for Maker's Mark. It felt too heavy."

Quinn shook his head. "And I thought we couldn't teach an old dog new tricks."

We embraced. "And I've certainly had my share of tricks."

Quinn signaled for the bartender to bring him a glass of the same wine, and then rubbed his hands together and looked around the hotel bar. "Is she bringing the bull-dyke girlfriend with her?"

I shrugged my shoulders.

"Curtis, I have this image of her wearing a blue uniform, with a billy club on one hip and a pistol on the other, and missing several fingers."

"She's a lesbian, not a prison guard."

"From what you tell me, it sounds like she should be in prison."

In fact, Mother said she had done time.

The bartender brought him his drink and set out a bowl of peanuts and, interesting enough, a tier of hard-boiled eggs. Quinn and I just looked at them for a moment, blankly.

"Quinn, are you still dating the pony?"

"Nope, I'm out of the saddle." He slipped off his barstool and adjusted his pants. "I should have taken your advice weeks ago and told Colt that we just weren't a match. Instead, it dragged on and on and has just kinda fizzled out."

Truth be told, I was glad he didn't listen to me. I learned the hard way that that wouldn't have been the most sensitive way to handle it.

"Curtis, your silence over Eric is driving me insane. What went down, besides you?"

I doubled over with laughter. "You know, Quinn, you really are funny."

"Of course I am," he said, grinning ear to ear. "Now tell me what happened."

I was tempted to share everything with him, the good stuff

and the bad, but then I heard Magda's voice telling me to hold on to it. It was mine. "I wish him well."

He took a sip of his drink. "Translation: He's an asshole?"

"No, not at all. The best I can say is that we were honest with each other."

"Look!" shouted Quinn as he pointed to the sweeping staircase. "Is that your mother in the dark sunglasses?"

She was climbing that staircase like Mary Tyrone in *Long Day's Journey into Night*. She'd do anything for attention.

"Mrs. J. over here," Quinn said as he opened his arms. "And where's the girlfriend?"

"Hello, boys."

She embraced both of us.

"Mother, why in God's name are you wearing sunglasses at this time of night?"

She took off her shades, revealing not one black eye but two.

"Mother!" I exclaimed.

Quinn put his hand to mouth. "Geez, Mrs. J., what happened?"

"The bitch hit me." She waved down the bartender as she slipped her glasses back on. "What's your name?"

"Dan," he replied.

"Danny, be a doll and make me a gin martini. No, make it a double straight up, very dry, with three olives."

"Robbie did this to you?" I asked.

Mother told us that after hearing that I went bowling, she and Robbie developed an itch to play. So after a few games they sat down at the bar for a drink.

At one point, Robbie went off to the ladies' room, and when she came back she saw my mother talking to a pretty blonde. They were innocently chitchatting about each other's bowling scores and—strike—Robbie hit the pretty young blonde. And then—strike—she hit my mother. The other gal fell to the floor, and my mother was helping her up when—strike—Robbie hit her in the other eye."

I shook my head, knowing we were all going to end up on a TV courtroom show.

Quinn held her hand. "I hope you aren't going to see her again, Mrs. J."

She slipped off her glasses again and showed us up close how swollen her eyes were. "Darling, right now I can't see anybody, literally."

"At least you haven't lost your sense of humor, Mother."

"Are you going to press charges?" Quinn asked, with hopeful anticipation of the drama.

"No, I'm throwing that fish back into the sea. The Jenkins name has been dragged through enough dirt as it is. I'm going to let bygones be bygones."

"Good for you, Mother." I raised my glass. "I'd like to propose a toast." They raised their glasses. "Here's to being single. No, here's to being happily single. Cheers."

"Skoal," added Quinn.

"Bottoms up," nodded my mother.

We had clinked glasses and taken sips when my mother took two small, identically wrapped packages out of her purse and gave one to each of us.

She winked as we both tore them open.

"Curtis, I know I've been batting zero in the matchmaking department, but this time I know I've found both of you the perfect partners."

I read the front of the package. "Grow a boyfriend." We all cackled.

Quinn read, "If you can't get a date, then grow the perfect mate."

It was a small rubber man, and, when added to water, it said that it would grow to six times its original size.

"Six times? I'm jealous," Quinn said as we all howled.

On the back it said that the boyfriend would slowly shrink when removed from water. Then you can grow him again and again.

We couldn't breathe, we were laughing so hard.

"Wait, there's more," Quinn shouted. "It says that the boyfriend will begin to grow after two hours and will reach full size in seventy-two hours."

"I can't wait that long," I declared.

With that, we all squealed in hysterics.

Just then, a man from across the bar shouted something at us that I hadn't heard in a long time: "Faggots!"

That certainly ruined the mood. The three of us were silent. The bartender was in the back, and no one was near us at the bar.

My mother slowly got off her stool, spread her legs wide, putting her hands on her hips, and asked him to repeat what he had said.

He looked at me and then at Quinn, and in a vicious whisper, he repeated, *"Faggots."* And then he turned his back to us.

In a flash, my mother grabbed one of the hard-boiled eggs and threw it as hard as she could, hitting him on the back of the head.

Something cracked, but it wasn't the egg. The man sat there motionless. Then he fell off the stool.

The three of us ran around the bar and saw him passed out on the floor.

"That egg was awfully heavy," my mother admitted.

I picked it up and knew right away that they weren't hardboiled—they were made of marble.

"Come on, boys," my mother said softly. "Let's eat somewhere else."

We threw money down for the drinks, grabbed our coats and our "boyfriends," and scurried out of the Paradise Hotel bar, giggling all the way.

≷ ≶

After dinner, the partners in crime sailed downtown to party, and I headed straight home. I had an early appointment with Magda the next day and wanted a clear head.

I was eager to tell her how things ended up with Eric and that I was okay with it. And that I was slowly but nonjudgmentally accepting my mother's newly disclosed (to me) sexual preference. I thought to myself, *As long as she's happy, that's what counts.*

But this time I didn't run to Magda's. I walked slowly, savoring the feeling of being at peace and in the moment. As I turned onto Riverside Drive, there was a large moving van in front of her building. Men were coming out with the last pieces of furniture as I scooted through the front door.

You know you are a true New Yorker when the first thing you think about when you see someone moving is whether or not the apartment is still available.

I climbed the stairs, expecting to hear Emily-Mae's annoying bark, but I heard nothing. In fact, when I reached Magda's floor, her heavy oak door was open.

"Hello?" I asked tentatively.

I slowly walked in and my heart sank. Her apartment was totally empty. I rushed to the front window, but the moving van was already leaving. What had happened?

I started back down the staircase when the door on the second landing creaked open. A waft of beef stew emanated from the apartment. This time, as I looked at it, the door did not slam shut. An elderly woman, severely stooped over and holding a big wooden spoon, stuck her head out.

"You looking for Magda?" Mrs. French asked in a raspy voice.

Still dazed, I said, "Yes, we had a ten-o'clock appointment."

"She's gone," she said abruptly, as she started back into her apartment.

Confused, I asked her, "I know she went to Poland, but she's not back yet?"

She turned back to me with an annoyed look. "She went to Poland, alright. She went in a pine box."

Stunned, I just looked at her.

"Magda died almost a month ago."

I leaned against the staircase banister for support.

"She was taking down drapes in her bedroom. Fell off her stepladder and hit her head. Broke her neck." Mrs. French ran a cooking spoon across her throat. "They said she didn't suffer."

My eyes were already welling with tears.

"There was a memorial here." She pinched her nose with her fingers and made a funny face. "Everyone brought their pets."

"I wished that I had known."

"I called everyone in Magda's address book, but maybe since you had only visited a few times, she didn't have you in it yet. Obviously, you weren't seeing her professionally."

I looked at her oddly.

"Because you came alone." She started to close her door.

"Well, why wouldn't I?"

"Because she was a vet."

I paused to think, and I still couldn't put it all together. "A veteran?"

"No, Magda was a veterinarian," Mrs. French barked.

A *veterinarian*? The animal pictures on the mantle. I had looked at her diplomas hanging on the walls, but they were too faded to decipher. And there was the stainless-steel table.

"Yup, she was a vet. Actually, a retired vet. But still helped people out here and there."

"Yes," I whispered in a daze. "She helped me out tremendously."

"What was that?" she asked, putting the wooden spoon up

to her ear. "Speak up, young man."

"Nothing."

She tried shutting her door, but something was in the way.

"Damn it." Suddenly, Emily-Mae appeared at the door.

"Just my luck, I end up with this creature. I can't take care of her, and I don't want her. Sending her down to the pound. They'll put her out of her misery. The thing won't eat. Must be depressed."

I knelt down to Emily-Mae and held out my hand. She sniffed it and immediately started barking.

"Well, what do ya know. She must recognize you."

⋛   ⋚

Still stunned at the news of Magda's death, I walked up Broadway toward my apartment. I wasn't paying much attention to anything. I do recall an ambulance screaming by, a woman yelling at her child, and car horn blowing.

I desperately wanted to hold on to the last image I had of Magda. She was wearing a short-sleeved blue print dress, a pair of blue pumps, and a beautiful turquoise bracelet. The kind you would find in Santa Fe.

And then, suddenly, I remembered something she said to me during our first session together.

"If you want to continue working with me, I suggest you have a minimum of one date per week and we will see each other every two weeks, until you find a man."

She left too soon. I thought Eric was the one. But like so many other fruits looking bright and colorful, who are firm to the touch and hoping to be picked and taken home for keeps, I too was ultimately put back on the shelf, because I'm slightly bruised and a bit too mushy on the inside.

Stopping at a red light, a man tapped me on my shoulder.

"It just peed on me," he said with an out-of-town accent.

"What?" I asked as I looked down.

"Your dog just peed on my shoe."

Although her gaze was veering off to the left, Emily-Mae seemed to look up at me proudly.

"Oh, gosh, I'm so sorry. She's been under a lot of stress. But it's a good thing. It means she likes you."

Finally, I looked at the man's face. "Hey, you're the guy from Paris. Paris, Texas."

"And you're the one who ran into the bus. Dell here." We shook hands.

"I'm Curtis." I searched my coat pocket for tissue. "Let me find something to clean up your shoe with."

"It's okay," he said, smiling. "I was hoping that you would call me."

"I'm sorry, Dell. I've been busy and—"

"No pressure." He looked apprehensively at Emily-Mae. "So, what kind of dog is that?"

I paused too long, racking my brain.

Finally, he asked, "It is a dog, isn't it?"

"Yes. I laughed. "It's a Brussels . . . it's a Brussels . . . it's an Emily-Mae."

"I've never seen one like her."

As Dell reached down to pet her, she growled, baring her needles at him.

"Emily-Mae, where are your manners?" I petted her head. "She's blind and deaf and pretty cranky."

"I would be, too." Dell chuckled. "She's an old-timer. How long have you had her?"

I looked at my watch. "Going on ten minutes. She was my shrin—she was my friend Magda's dog. But she's passed away, and so I've adopted her."

"You're a good friend, Curtis." The three of us casually strolled up Broadway together. "So, what do you do for a living?"

"I'm a writer."

He stopped and turned to me, saying, "I love to read." Dell said it so enthusiastically and with such a huge smile that it made me chuckle inside. "And do you live around here?"

We resumed walking. "Yes, and you?"

"No, out in Brooklyn. Some of the guys on the team and I volunteer up here at the Boys Club."

I thought that was very admirable. "What kind of team are you with?"

"If I told you I was a member of a real famous sports club, would you hold it against me?"

"Hell, no. Is it football?" Now this time I was the one bursting with enthusiasm. "I watch it all the time. I especially like the intermissions."

Dell let loose a huge laugh. "Let's just say that I'm a professional ballplayer."

I turned to him and smiled. "I'm a terrific athletic supporter."

We both laughed and talked as Emily-Mae pulled us along, bumping into anything and everything she could bark at, the blind leading the blind.

Just then, we came upon the bag lady.

"Any change, sir?" She held out her paper coffee cup with her brown-leathered hand. "Any change today?"

I dug deep into my pocket, pulled out a twenty-dollar bill, and placed it in her cup. And for the first time, I replied out loud, "Yes, ma'am. There is a change today."